The Scrapple Eater

Byron Grush

Published in the United States by Broadhorn Publishing, Delavan, WI

ISBN-10: 0-9985454-0-6
ISBN-13: 978-0-9985454-0-0

Front cover image derived from "Mausoleums in the Mount Moriah Cemetery in Philadelphia," by Smallbones
Back cover image: "The Professor," photographer unknown.

Author's Preface

Stories have to come from somewhere. Windsor McCay, the animator and cartoonist of *Little Nemo in Slumberland,* penned an earlier comic strip called *Dreams of A Rarebit Fiend* about a man who ate too much of that exotic cheese dish before bedtime. This caused him to have some very strange dreams, indeed. Inspiration sometimes comes from unusual places.

Our main character, a young man named Jefferson, seems to be obsessed with graveyards, and with eating scrapple. He has some troubling dreams. He thinks he may have a ghost. Could it be that this strange concoction of uncommon animal parts gives rise to visions and dreams? Or, as Harry Houdini once asked, do the dead return? Where do we go when we die? If we go somewhere, can we come back? Many of the ghostly manifestations alluded to in the story are based on local legends. It seems that ghosts like Western Pennsylvania.

Now, I haven't been devouring excess scrapple (see the story for the recipe), but I have been doing a lot of research into my ancestors on my father's side who settled in Pennsylvania, near where the story takes place. The directions to the cemetery in the first chapter are, in fact, directions to a real cemetery where the majority of the graves are from a family named Grush. I haven't discovered any hereditary ties to these people, in spite of the rarity of the name.

Other cemeteries mentioned in the story also exist. Older cemeteries, a good source of information for would-be genealogists like myself, are beginning to be "walked" by dedicated volunteers. Inscriptions are recorded and sometimes, photographs are taken. My utmost appreciation goes out to these "walkers" without whom we would be at the mercy of certain commercial enterprises who require payment for data, even though it is in the public domain (like census records). How can you copyright history? Obviously, you can't.

I'm reminded of a story by E. B. White called "The Door" in which a man is told, "We could take your name and send it to you." Online ancestry companies do just that. They collect your data by helping you construct an online family tree, then make the information you gave them available to others for a fee. Thanks to the internet and the willingness of amateur researchers to share data, there is a lot you can learn about your ancestors without having to support vampiristic corporations.

Now that my rant is over I should pen a disclaimer: I know nothing about Quantum Mechanics. Just the same, it is intriguing to apply certain of its theories to the realm of the supernatural. Perhaps, Schrödinger's cat has nine lives. Perhaps the Spiritualist's vision of the afterlife is a kind of parallel theory to the idea of multiple universes. Perhaps when we die we only enter into a different dream than the one where we dreamed we were alive.

One of my favorite authors, Sir Arthur Conan Doyle, was convinced that Spiritualism was valid. He had an ongoing conflict with Harry Houdini who spent a great deal of time and trouble debunking Spiritualist charlatans. Of course, there were many who believed that Houdini had supernatural powers. Well, I've personally never seen a ghost...or a flying saucer or any other psychic phenomenon. And I do eat scrapple, whenever I'm in Pennsylvania. But I'm ready and willing to believe.

1

The Old Cemetery

Located in Paint Township, Somerset County, PA. From Somerset Street in Windber, take 17th Street (which turns into Railroad Street after a block) for 2.2 miles past the coal tipple. On the left side of the road is a paved access road leading into the mine area. Off to the right side of this paved road is a small clearing and then the tree line. The cemetery is located within the tree line about 100 meters up the hill and can be difficult to find.   —directions to the old cemetery.

A broken slab of granite was set over the rusted iron doors, its chiseled inscription, "Eureka No. 40 1904," still visible under a thin layer of lichen and mold. Jefferson used the tripod for this picture, the morning light was shy of this hillock; branches of dead trees encircled the closed entrance to the old mine now, keeping the site in perpetual shade. Jefferson wondered what working in that mine had been like. Judging from the size of the doorway and its proximity to the top of the small hill, the ceiling must have been inches above the heads of the miners.

There was a company town just up the road. Rows of small, identical houses with peeling paint, sloped roofs and rickety looking porches lined either side of the narrow dirt road. A slate dump was nearby, looming over the little town like a dark gray miniature

1

mountain in a ghostly fairy tale. People still lived here, he supposed. Did their children play on the gob pile and climb on the splintering shacks? Thank goodness the mine itself was sealed!

Jefferson now moved closer to the tipple. This was a large building constructed of concrete with upper stories framed in wood and sheeted with metal. A large cone-shaped device dangled from the underbelly of the beast. This was used, Jefferson had been told by the "old-timer" who had shown him around the abandoned site earlier this morning, to wash, crush, rewash the coal and separate it from refuse. He could imagine the sounds and the smells issuing from this processing plant—and drifting irreverently down into the town.

Jefferson loved photographing ruins, the left-over relics of humanity's insane rush toward riches, and its ultimate failure. He loved the rust, the crumbling stone, the rotting wood, the shadows of long gone people that still lurked (you could see them if you knew where to look) like ghosts, the futile attempts of mother nature to reclaim the battle ground where mankind had raped the land.

Sickly looking weeds poked through cracks in the tumbled foundation of the company office. Dead and dried vines wound around the metal supports of the tipple like decorations hastily hung for an All Hallows' Eve event attended by no one. There was no grass, no dirt…only a fine carpet of coal dust. Jefferson considered climbing the slag heap to get a bird's eye view of the town, but he had a cemetery to find and to photograph. If the directions he'd found on line were accurate, it should be within walking distance of where he had left the car. Old mining sites were a good source of inspiration, but cemeteries were like meat and potatoes to a starving photog.

He had happened on the idea while researching his ancestors. That had been difficult at first. His parents had been distinctly silent on the subject. He had barely known his paternal grandfather who had passed away when Jefferson was five, and his grandmother had already been entering senility. No hope there, only an old family bible with a page torn out of it where the family tree had once been penned. On his mother's side there were no living grandparents. The few cousins he had weren't interested in heritage.

Now, however, there were numerous web sites that posted useful, searchable data like census and military records. And the locations of cemeteries. There were thousands upon thousands of old cemeteries with the names, dates of birth and death of the interred etched in stone. The only problem was that you had to visit the grave yard in order to read the inscriptions. The quick needed to go to dead. And the quick would need to take a camera. Jefferson decided to become a cemetery walker; he would photograph headstones and post the photographs on a web site.

Jefferson liked the "Ca-clack!" sound his digital camera made. It was supposed to simulate the shutter of an old 35mm reflex camera. It was comforting both in assuring him that he had, indeed, taken the shot, and in traversing the schism between the technology of today and the certain nostalgia he felt about the photography of the past. He remembered the red-orange glow of the safelight, the pungent smell of fixer and developer in trays laid haphazardly on a board in his parents' bathroom, the brown stains on his fingers.

He had gotten a developing outfit for his twelfth birthday: plastic trays for prints and a tank for negatives, a small box with a light bulb inside to expose the photo paper—it had a little hinged door you fastened with a metal clamp that sometimes pinched your fingers. His first subject had been the family dog, a grumpy old dachshund that nobody liked. He produced a trick photo of the wiener dog with a head at each end. Photography became, for Jefferson, a way of asserting himself and of transforming an otherwise dismal reality into precious, frozen instances of insight.

Now he walked through the clearing toward the trees. It was as if nature and mankind had drawn a line, saying, "this side is mine, that side is yours." The ground angled upward and he climbed. He entered the thick wood, stumbling through the undergrowth, pushing aside saplings that barred his passage. The description had said that the cemetery wasn't easy to find; it wasn't. Once into the thicket the outside world no longer existed; even the sky disappeared. Every turn further frustrated his meager sense of direction. Finally, he saw a horizontal line ahead in the jumble of branches and twigs: a sort of fence made from wire stretched between cement posts—a futile attempt to separate the burial ground from the woods.

He brushed aside the dead leaves and branches that partially hid a weathered grave marker. He set up the camera. It had been more artistic the way he had found it, but then, that wasn't the point. He needed a clear picture of each monument in the cemetery for posting on his web site. Jefferson thought of himself as a sort of a nouveau resurrectionist: a digital grave robber digging up data for amateur genealogists who were putting together their family trees. Now he would photograph each headstone and copy whatever was readable in his notebook to annotate the images he would upload. His specialty was old, abandoned cemeteries where forgotten ancestors lay beneath deteriorating marble and granite, where history was signified in stone that slowly dissolved in the rain and the sleet— words crying out to be archived with electronic ones and zeros on his server's hard drive. If he made a few bucks selling advertisements and subscriptions to his web site, well, that was a plus.

There were only a handful of graves here, but the dates were all well into the nineteenth century. No fresh flowers adorned them. There was not even a plastic wreath or a tattered flag stuck into the soft ground to signify deference from the living. The descendents had moved on, their great-great grandparents forgotten or lost to them in eroded time. A singular loneliness enveloped the remote hillock where the cemetery sat, sheltered from the road by the dense thicket. Crows and turkey vultures were its only visitors.

As Jefferson moved from grave to grave, ca-clacking and writing in a spiral-bound notebook, the heels of his hiking boots left half-moon impressions that would weather away along with the "beloved son of" and the "our sweet angel" inscriptions on the markers. He found a grave with the first name "Jefferson" but with an obliterated surname, the date over a century ago. Funny, he thought, Jefferson is not that common a name. It gave a person an eerie feeling to see their own name on a tombstone like that.

Here lay Joseph _____, prominent farmer of Rummel, aged 70 years, died on March 20 after several month's illness. Next to him was a broken stone, the name Peter barely visible, and the dates: b. Nov. 17, 1805 d. Jan. 8, 1876—husband (it said) of Eve. There were two weathered stones behind this, their chalk white silhouettes leaning against each other, inseparable for eternity: Daniel and Mary Ann. And behind this, a smaller marker with the inscription, "Infant Son b: 19 Sep 1875 d: 16 Nov 1875"—the death of children always made Jefferson shiver.

A number of markers had been broken and pieces lay in disarray on the ground. This happened in many of the older cemeteries where the head stones were composed of softer materials, when moisture invaded the porous stone and froze in winter's bitter cold. The fallen slabs, like misshapen puzzle pieces, called for reconstruction, a resurrection not unlike that yearned for by the souls tucked away below in the wormy earth. Broken grave stones always made Jefferson think of Shelly's poem about Ozymandias:

> *"My name is Ozymandias, king of kings:*
> *Look on my works, ye Mighty, and despair!"*
> *Nothing beside remains. Round the decay*
> *Of that colossal wreck, boundless and bare*
> *The lone and level sands stretch far away.*

The stones, yielding only the barest statistics, hinted at stories untold. This one, was he a merchant? A farmer? Had he a large family? Did a son go off to war? That one, perhaps a preacher, struggling to sustain a dwindling congregation, fearing the Devil and his works. A mother of twelve children—six lost to fevers that burned, food that was tainted, accidents in barn or field. A miner, walking home to those little row houses, black from coal dust. A lawyer fighting to keep his client, an escaped slave, from the penetrating tentacles of the South.

Another inscription caused him to pause. "Elizabeth, 16 yrs, Taken Too Soon," it said. "Died October 8, 1849." There were many infant deaths in those days of course, but this was something else. A young girl struck down in her prime. By what? Typhoid? Tuberculosis? Scarlet fever? There were so many diseases, treatable today, that had eluded the physicians of the nineteenth century. It was troublesome.

He tried to visualize this Elizabeth. Dark hair? Auburn? Golden locks that tumbled across her bared shoulders (Jefferson liked bared shoulders, delicate necks, unadorned throats). He decided on the gold, and a full-skirted summer frock with petticoats showing as she rustled along a garden path or along a bubbling stream. Had she known that other resident of this grave yard, that Jefferson Last-name-obscured? Did they play together as children? Grow into adolescence together? Did they experience the first blush of love? Then she became sick and died. He mourned and never married. He went to war, was killed in battle, his body shipped back to be buried next to his only true love…

Jefferson was a hopeless romantic. He couldn't help fantasizing about the dearly departed. Perhaps it was the lack of detail in their stories that piqued to him. He would fill in the spaces with imaginary scenarios that suited his often morbid, rarely hopeful outlook on life. There were many untold stories here, now covered with a blanket of dried leaves and twigs—the province of squirrels, the dominion of decay.

Jefferson negotiated the steep slope down to his car, stowing the camera and collecting the vase of fresh geraniums he had brought. He returned to the cemetery and placed it on the grave of the 16 year old girl, Elizabeth. He often left flowers when he worked cemeteries. It made him feel closer to the process of life and death. He may have been removed in time from them, but these people he never knew and would never meet seemed more real when acknowledged with this simple ritual. He stood in silence for a moment, not because of any religious conviction, but to savor the mortal essence of the place.

2

Lou's Diner

Sitting on the side of the highway, gleaming in the noonday sun like a silver smile, the diner, or dinar as some people spelled it, beckoned to Jefferson. The long narrow building lined with stainless steel siding had a row of windows across its street-facing side that was reminiscent of the coach cars of streamlined trains. The signage perched atop of the diner had a characteristic art deco style, with sweeping curves and red block letters announcing the name of the establishment: Lou's Diner.

Jefferson turned the steering wheel of his Subaru sharply and slid onto the gravel parking lot. The diner with its shining siding (it reminded him of a rocket ship from a Flash Gordon movie serial) presented a curious contrast to the otherwise drab Allegheny mining country with its slag heaps and unpainted wooden buildings. He had headed south and west toward Shanksville where United Airlines Flight 93 had crashed on September eleventh, 2001. He wanted to photograph the memorial there but the lure of the diner and a growling stomach took precedence.

The inside felt bigger than the outside suggested; a tall, arched ceiling with hanging, milk-glass lighting globes exaggerated the cave-like space. On the window side were several small booths with Formica table tops. Across the narrow aisle from the booths was a long counter. Along that swivel-topped stools were fastened to the tiled floor. At intervals along the counter top one could find built-in racks for napkins, salt, pepper, sugar, and plastic mustard and ketchup bottles. At the end of the counter nearest the door was a glass case whose shelves held an array of pies: cocoanut-cream, cherry, apple and shoo-fly pie. Everywhere was shining white enamel, strips of stainless steel molding, and other vintage materials that spoke of a bygone era.

Perched on a vinyl topped stool at the counter, Jefferson was inundated by a variety of extraordinary fragrances: the aroma of bubbling hot coffee, the scent of bacon frying, the acrid steam of hash browns and the rich sizzling smell of fresh eggs hitting the grill. There was no backroom kitchen here; the flat-top grill was right behind the counter. Jefferson watched as the cook cracked egg shells with one hand while working a spatula under hash browns with the other. He ordered bacon and eggs, toast and coffee.

"Pannhass?" asked the counter man.

"Yes. Everything but the oink," replied Jefferson. Scrapple, or pannhass as the Pennsylvania Dutch called it, was a favorite indulgence of his whenever he traveled through Pennsylvania. Its gritty, oily texture and slightly spicy tang were as exotic as the parts of the hog used to prepare it—parts he didn't care to ponder. It had been his father's personal choice for breakfast. This had irritated his mother who thought it a lower class cuisine and frankly, pretty disgusting. But liver, brain, heart and various bits of porcine offal had a dark and intense flavor that suited both his palate as well as his philosophy. Use everything. Experience everything. Embrace all aspects of life, especially those that connected life with death.

He remembered his father's stories of growing up on the farm, watching *his* father, Jefferson's grandfather, throwing the discarded bits of a freshly butchered hog into a huge metal pot and boiling the contents down. The entire head would gape up out of the pot at his father. Ears and the tail and bits of skin would float to the surface. The rectum was a bit chewy and was sometimes left out. They would skim off most of the fat and pull out the bones, mixing cornmeal and herbs into the broth until it thickened. Larger chunks of meat were minced by hand and then returned to the pot. The mush-like concoction was cooled, rolled thin and sliced, then pan fried in lard until browned and crispy on the outside. Jefferson's father would salivate when telling the story.

When Jefferson's order was placed before him he queried the counterman about the cemetery he had just left. The counterman responded that he had never heard of local cemetery like the one Jefferson described. And there was not much else to tell. Jefferson then asked about any descendents that might still live in the area. The man just shook his head.

"I recall they was a couple families of Brethren. Lived all together and had a hill farm. Cholera wiped them out. Ever last one."

"Some pretty young?"

"The youngest were the weakest. Terrible epidemics those days."

Jefferson started to think about Elizabeth, 16 years, taken too soon. What did he remember about the date, 1849? The California gold rush? He fired up his iPhone and googled 1849. James K. Polk was president—the first U. S. President to have his photograph taken. That was interesting. The Irish Potato Famine. Hmm. The Astor Opera House Riots in New York City where thousands clashed because of the rivalry between British and American Shakespearean actors. A broken Mississippi River levee flooding New Orleans. Nothing about a cholera epidemic. There was one in 1832 and another in 1873 but Elizabeth would have missed both of those. Of course, a disaster in a little place like Somerset County probably didn't rate for the history books. Until 9/11, that was.

Jefferson shoveled scrapple into his mouth and bit down on something hard. Indifferent, he spit it out and kept eating. The bacon and eggs were spectacular and the scrapple—divine! You couldn't get food this good in Poughkeepsie. He had just gestured with his cup for a refill of coffee when he heard a voice behind him say, "You could ask Betty Snyder."

"Pardon me?" said Jefferson, swiveling on his stool toward the voice. It had come from a small gray-haired man in a booth by the window. He was sitting with an equally small woman wearing a red babushka. The woman's smile exposed a missing tooth as she said, "Oh yes, Betty would know all about it."

"May I join you?" asked Jefferson. Receiving nods to the affirmative from the odd old couple, Jefferson slid into the booth beside the old man. "Who is Betty Snyder?" he asked.

"She's the local historian. Knows all about the early settlers, the miners and the farmers that lived here. She'd know what happened to your people."

"Well, they're not my... uh, that would be very helpful. Can you tell me where I might find this Betty Snyder?"

"She'd be at the Historical building. That's up on Somerset Street."

"No, hun. It's on 15th," said the woman.

"What? They moved it?"

"No. Always been there. You just look for it tucked away behind the old municipal building. Can't miss it. A big old house with double porches. Sign'll say 'museum' an Miss Snyder will probably be there today."

"You sure it's not on Somerset?"

Jefferson thanked the couple, who were still bickering about the location of the museum, and went back to the counter where his bill, a grease-stained light-green piece of paper with $1.99 scribbled on it in pencil, waited for him next to his cup of now cold coffee. He put three singles on the counter and left the diner, breathing in one last aromatic smell of the kind of cooking that existed nowhere else on earth except in a diner.

He'd come through Windber after leaving the cemetery but hadn't taken much notice of the town. It was an actual town, in contrast to the patch town of identical small houses he had seen near the mine. There had been nine deep mines in the area, most having cheap housing for the miners; most were closed now. In Windber proper, however, one could stroll through what was now being called a Historic District, dating to 1897 when the Berwind White Coal Company had laid out a grid of streets between the Big Paint Creek on the south and the steep wooded hills to the north. In the country surrounding the coal-rich Windber Field there had still been farms run by Pennsylvania Dutch settlers—settlers like those buried in the cemetery Jefferson had just photographed. Not much was left of these farms; the area had become a Mecca for coal mining, lumber and brick-making.

In the Windber commercial district there was a company store (the Eureka Department Store which had branches in the patch towns) and a municipal building, the corporate headquarters of the mining company, a bank and trust (run by the mining company), a hotel and several churches, all interspersed with working class houses. The commercial buildings were of red brick, manufactured in the area, and made in the popular Italian Renaissance Revival style of the day. The workers' houses were a cut above those in the patch towns, but still were modest wooden structures often needing a fresh coat of paint.

Just north of the downtown was The Hill: originally an exclusive residential area composed of Queen Anne and Colonial Revival houses—not quite mansions, but substantial in size, design and upkeep—where company officials and professionals could enjoy an idyllic retreat along tree-lined avenues, away from the dirt and grim of the coal industry they had fostered. Windber had never been subject matter for, say, the illustrations of Norman Rockwell, but it projected a kind of classic feeling of nostalgia in those who visited…Jefferson was not immune.

Back in town, Jefferson drove up and down 15th Street, looking for the museum. He missed it twice. Then he spotted a small, hand-painted sign: "Windber Area Museum and Historic Shaffer House, hours Saturday and Sunday, 1 PM to 4 PM. Donations are gratefully accepted." It was a lovingly restored house with a front porch and overhead balcony that reminded Jefferson of the houses on Bourbon Street in New Orleans, except instead of wrought iron railings it had balustrades of turned wooden balusters, painted chalky white. He could almost imagine a small Victorian era child climbing on them.

He peeked in the window. The front room was full of period furniture, brightly patterned rugs, ornate frames showing off portraits of bearded and mustached men and prim, elegantly dressed women (everyone seemed to be frowning). There was a collection of old violins hung on one wall and framed, brown-turned pages from old newspapers on another. As today was neither Saturday nor Sunday, there was no one around. He turned to go when he noticed a piece of paper which had been taped to the front door but which had come partially loose and was flapping in the slight breeze. He straightened it out. It gave a phone number to call for inquiries about the museum during those hours in which it was closed (which seemed to be most of the time).

Jefferson punched the number into his cell using his fingers—he had never mastered the technique of thumb dialing so popular with the younger generation. When a woman answered, he explained that he was trying to get in touch with a Betty Snyder who, he hoped, could shed some light on a sort of mystery about an old grave yard he had visited. The woman replied that in fact, she was Betty Snyder. Could he arrange to meet with her? Today if possible? Betty Snyder responded by giving directions to her place of residence—not very far from where he was, she said. After Jefferson ended the call he shook his head. How did she know he wasn't some kind of a mass murderer? What a world!

Byron Grush

3

Betty Snyder's House

It was one of those elegant old Victorian houses, the ones they called the "painted ladies." Indeed, this one had been freshly painted in pinks and greens with red and purple accents. An abundance of bric-a-brac greeted Jefferson as he climbed the wooden stairs to the wrap-around porch. A large gray cat scurried out from under a porch swing and ran between his feet, awakened from its afternoon nap by his passage. He twisted the old fashioned doorbell, surprised at the volume of its clamor. Loud enough to wake the dead, he mused to himself.

Betty Snyder was not at all what Jefferson had expected. To begin with, she was young, perhaps about his own age, the late side of twenty. He wouldn't have said he was dazzled by her beauty, her long hair shining black like coal, or the hypnotic gaze of her smiling eyes. Instead, he would have said he wasn't prone to love at first sight, nor lust nor fascination for that matter. He would tell you he had maintained a certain ambivalence toward her attractive qualities, the way she stood on the porch, her weight on one foot, one hand on her hip while the other brushed back hair wind-blown by gusts. She was tall, with a lithe figure that reminded Jefferson of willow trees in spring. And he was, against his will and better judgment, completely captivated.

She led him through the entry hall across a thick carpet runner decorated with a pattern of intertwined ostrich feathers. He saw that her feet were bare, her toe nails painted black. In the sitting room heavy maroon drapes framed floor-to-ceiling windows. Would he like tea? Would he sit here on the velvet-covered chair with the carved wooden arms? Was the room too warm? She could open a window. She's not quite beautiful, he thought, but really pretty. The cat entered the room and began brushing against his leg.

She sat on a dark yellow, flower-patterned, chintz-upholstered davenport (quite out of place in the old-fashioned setting of her vintage home) with her legs curled under her. She waited for him to speak—he had requested the interview, after all. But somehow Jefferson felt tongue-tied. He seemed to have forgotten his mission in coming here. It was something about a cemetery, wasn't it?

"So you run the museum here?" he finally said. What a stupid, inane question, he thought. What am I, a school boy enamored with his first grade teacher? But she didn't chide him or give even a hint of amusement.

"Oh, no, I only volunteer on weekends."

"Well, ah, the reason I called…I'm a photographer. And a researcher…sort of. I document old graveyards for genealogical purposes. I was up at a cemetery near the Number 40 mine and I found a grave…well, there was this girl…"

"A young girl taken too soon…before her time. The inscription spoke to you. But it left you wondering about the girl. Who she was. Why she died."

"Yes. Something like that. Her age was 16. Was there an epidemic or something? The year was 1849."

She answered his questions about the old cemetery. Yes, there had been a cholera epidemic but it hadn't killed everyone. Some simply moved away. As she talked, her soft voice seemed to mesmerize him, lull him into a pleasant reverie in which he could see the old countryside as it had once been. Sheep on the hills, crops on the low lands. Soon the coal companies would come to scrape and scar and eat away the land like maggots boring beneath the feathers of dead birds—but not yet. Now there was the sweet smell of heather and fresh cut timothy, scintillating breezes full of bird song. He was transported back in time.

"Beth, wait up!" he called after the young girl running up Ford's Lane. She broke stride and turned her head, raven tresses swinging, a few wispy hairs caught between her lips. He hurried to catch up as she leaned against the rail fence, one leg propped on the bottom rail, exposing a dirty knee.

"Hello, Jeffy," she chimed, her voice bright as carriage bells.

"Hello, Beth! Where ya going in such a rush?" He thought that her simple black dress with its long row of buttons was an odd uniform for such playful scampering up a country lane. "Why you still wearing that mourning? Your aunt's been gone…" (here he counted on his fingers) "…three, four weeks now."

"My mamma said…oh…you're asking a lot questions of me this morning! What are you, my big brother?"

"I'm your best friend. And I thought maybe we could go to Jason's pond for a swim. Summer's almost over."

"Jeffy! We're getting too old to go skinny dipping. And anyway, in case you haven't noticed, it's cold today!"

"Aw, Beth, it's just a little brisk, that's all."

"Would you like milk in that?"

"What?"

"Milk. Would you like milk in your tea?"

Jefferson nearly sloshed hot tea from the flowered china cup as he was jolted from his daydream. "I'm sorry, I blanked out there for a moment. No, no thank you. No milk."

"We were discussing cholera epidemics." Betty Snyder settled back onto the davenport. "The worst were in large city centers like New York or New Orleans. They say even the president, James Polk died from cholera. It was spread from contaminated drinking water or eating fish that swam in it. It was a bacterial infection that caused vomiting and diarrhea. People would become dehydrated and die in very short time. It must have been frightening."

He knelt by her bedside. Her eyes were sunken, her skin flaccid like soft dough. A stale odor permeated the room like dead fish on a beach. He was frantic. Where is the doctor? Please, God, don't take her. It was not the first person he had seen dying. Just the first love of his young life. Why don't they come? He held a cup of water to her lips. Her hands, wrinkled like an old women's rose to clasp his. Jeff, don't leave me. Beth, I'm here. Too young. We never.... His eyes were blurred from tears held back. He set his gaze on the sachet of potpourri lying on her pillow. In moments of extreme stress one focuses on individual objects, their importance magnified: an old rag doll collapsed on a ladder back chair, a wooden cross nailed above the bed, an open book, the page marked with a dried flower.

"I see you're looking at that photograph. That's my Great Uncle Ezra. It's from an old tintype I had enlarged." A stern looking old gentleman with abundant chin whiskers looked down at Jefferson from a carved oak frame.

"Looks like it might have been from a calotype. I'm a photographer, you know."

"You told me. Graveyards."

"I do photographs as an art form for my own pleasure, as well as documenting history. I'm not good enough to show, not yet anyhow. But that's my real love. When I have time I go out with a *real* camera filled with black and white film. This digital stuff is just for efficiency in the cemetery project. It's hard though, being on the go so much, to do darkroom work."

"You know, I have a project you might like. More lively than old graveyards. I found a box of glass negatives in an attic the other day. They're from the area. I want to make prints of them."

"Well, you could scan them. Or put them on a light box and rephotograph them. Reverse them using Photoshop."

"Yes, but I want paper prints directly from the negatives. I want to mount an exhibition of them at the museum. Would you help me do that?"

Would he help her do that? Jefferson couldn't believe this attractive young woman was giving him an opening—he was too shy himself to approach her in any nonprofessional manner, but he wanted—what did he want? Was he reading too much into this casual conversation? Probably.

"We'd need a darkroom, some trays, chemicals. And anyway, I'm headed for Shanksville," he blurted.

"There's a photographic supply house up in Johnstown. You could give me a list of what you need and I could get it overnighted. I'm sure we could rig up a darkroom. Please?"

"I guess I could come back in a day or two."

"Oh, thank you!" She sprang up and planted a kiss on his cheek. Jefferson reddened. There was no way he could spend the time making prints. But there was no way he could avoid coming back. No way he could not come back to be with her, especially if it involved a darkened room.

"May I see the glass negatives?" he asked.

Betty Snyder left the room and returned with a cardboard box which she placed on the coffee table. Jefferson began pulling plates from the box one by one and examining them. "These should be protected by storing them in paper envelopes. Envelopes that don't have glue on them…that can accelerate decomposition," he told her.

"Can you tell how old they are?"

"There are two kinds of glass negatives: wet plates and dry plates. The wet plates came first, probably between 1850 and 1870, roughly. In the wet plate process, the glass is coated with collodion. Now, that's a flammable concoction of cellulose nitrate and ether. You remember that the first motion picture films were nitrate based? They often spontaneously combusted. Dangerous stuff. Anyway, the collodion was dipped into a tray of silver nitrate, creating a light-sensitive emulsion on the plate. This all had to be done in total darkness. And the plate had to be exposed while it was still wet, and immediately developed. Traveling photographers had darkrooms built into their wagons. One of the most famous ones was Eadweard Muybridge.

"Around 1871 the dry plate was invented. The light-sensitive material was mixed with a gelatin and coated onto the glass plate and allowed to dry. It didn't need to be used immediately and was less delicate to handle. Obviously this made the wet plate obsolete."

"Can you tell which these are? That would help date them."

"Well, it's a little difficult. The wet plates usually have an uneven coating of emulsion and rough edges. The dry plates were made with thinner glass and the emulsion was more even. And the two types degrade differently. See here on this one, how the edges are flaking? My guess is that this one, at least, was a wet plate. You may have a variety of plates from different eras. Once we make prints we may be able to pin it down a little better by analyzing the subject matter."

"You mean what people are wearing, what the furniture looks like, if there are horses or motorcars? That is my area of expertise."

Jefferson was now committed to helping this woman. He wrote

out a list of supplies they would need: four developing trays, a safe light, archival printing paper, chemicals including a hypo-clearing agent, print flattening solution, and envelopes for storing the glass plates. He added non-latex gloves and a thermometer to the list.

"You'll need to dedicate a room with running water to the project. It should be as light tight as you can make it."

"This is exciting. Please hurry back from your photo shoot. I'll have everything ready for you."

As Jefferson pulled away from the house in his car he began to wonder: what was he getting himself into? He liked the free and easy existence he had, rambling around the country, exploring old cemeteries, taking pictures of subjects that interested him. He would certainly be tied up with the glass plates for several days. Stuck in a dark room with smelly chemicals. Of course, there was Betty…

4

The Crash Site

The robin's egg blue sign read, "Welcome to Shanksville, Home of the Vikings, A Friendly Little Town, Est. 1803." There wasn't much to it; about 245 in population, no motel, no restaurant that he could find. He had passed the crash site on the road into town, several miles back now, but he was tired. A meal and a motel were what he wanted. He parked and entered Ida's, a country store with an American flag on the wooden screen door. He asked the woman behind the counter where a meal and a room might be found. The woman, possibly Ida herself, told him to go up to 160, the road they called The Huckleberry Highway, and follow that to Central City. When he mentioned that he was interested in visiting the crash site the woman remarked:

"Oh Lordy, I should've guessed that. Not many people come by here except for that memorial. Terrible thing. Tragic. Well, in that case you'd be going out of your way to go to Central City. Turn left on Bridge Street and then right on Stutzmantown Road. Follow that all the way to Glades Pike and that'll take you right into Somerset. That'll be closer to the memorial. I think the motels are all up by the Turnpike north of town. You got your Burger King and whatnot too."

Jefferson thanked the woman and bought a newspaper and a

package of Hostess Twinkies from her before returning to his car. The next leg of his trip took him along a peaceful country road for about 10 miles, then into the town of Somerset. The population here was around 7,000; the proximity to the Pennsylvania Turnpike had given the historic town a bit of a growth spurt since its inception in 1795. It had been the scene of the Whiskey Rebellion of 1794.

Somerset was, of course, close to the 2001 crash site of United Airlines Flight 93, which had served to "put it on the map" (although it had been there all along). In 2002 nine miners had been trapped in the nearby Quecreek coal mine (all were rescued). The town also had a crater on Mars named for it. Other than that, there was nothing very exciting going on in Somerset.

Jefferson checked into the Days Inn and went in search of an eating establishment. There were all the usual fast food places near by: McDonald's, Wendy's, Ruby Tuesdays. But down on Center Avenue he struck gold: the Summit Diner. The square angles of the stand-alone metal-sheathed building and the classic neon "Diner" sign, all shouted Retro with a capital "R." It only dated to 1960 but it felt like 1940 and the food, well, Jefferson would compare the scrapple tomorrow morning to the faire he had gotten at Lou's. For now, he would go for a burger and fries and a thick milk shake.

All the good-old-boys were lined up on swivel seats along the counter, baseball caps pulled tightly over hair that could have used a trim but was conventionally short enough to pass at a church social. Many of them had a girth that challenged the structural integrity of the stools. Jefferson found an empty booth and slid into it. A waitress, actually wearing a pink outfit and white apron, came to inquire (in too loud and too high-pitched a voice), "Whatcha havin' hun?"

Jefferson ordered a pulled-pork sandwich with extra sauce on the side and fries. The burgers, he had noticed as he passed through the diner peering at people's half eaten meals, looked thin and greasy. Not all diners were created equal, he thought. But when his meal came he applied himself to it with a diligence appropriate to the best comfort food of his recent experience; a large heap of home-made French-fried potatoes, a small paper "bowl" of coleslaw, a glistening plump bun stuffed with shredded, slow-roasted pig drenched in a sauce that reminded him more of Saint Louis than of Richmond.

Back at his motel, Jefferson transferred the cemetery pictures to his laptop and began uploading them to his web site. Luckily this motel had free wifi—not all of them did. One by one he typed in the grave inscriptions he had copied into his notebook. There she was again: Elizabeth, died 16 years, taken too soon. And there was his namesake, Jefferson somebody, 1833 to an illegible date. Hopefully he hadn't died from cholera. Perhaps the Civil War had taken him? Perhaps Betty could tell him. Oh yes, Betty would know all about it.

The next morning he returned to the Summit Diner for fried eggs, toast and coffee…and, of course, scrapple. It was just right: crusty brown on the top and soft inside—not too thickly sliced. He could tell that buckwheat had been blended with the cornmeal making the panhaas seem pretty authentic. Some garlic and onion, of course, but with touches of coriander, nutmeg and clove to sweeten it a bit. Jefferson eased his over-easy eggs onto the top of the scrapple. His fork released the yellow yolk to run over the surface of the scrapple. Some people liked to pour maple syrup on their scrapple or even—gasp!—ketchup. Not so Jefferson. He wasn't a purist, but he knew what he liked. Maybe a little applesauce on the side, but never…never ketchup!

After devouring his breakfast, he drove back toward Shanksville. The crash site of United Airlines Flight 93 was at an abandoned strip mine, the Diamond T. Mine, several miles north of town. Jefferson drove up Lambertsville Road and turned sharply at Skyline Road where he saw a temporary sign reading "Flight 93" with the blue silhouette of an airliner and a red arrow pointing the way to the memorial. He located a parking lot next to the temporary memorial, a small square plot of land surrounded by a rail fence, and parked the Subaru.

He found there a granite monument of moderate size and off to one side, a wooden cross. Benches were arranged, Jefferson supposed, to mimic the seating of the airliner, and the names of the 40 passengers and crew were painted on them. These faced a row of small slate figures representing angels, the "Angels of Freedom," each labeled with the name of one of the 40 victims. There were plaques and collections of mementos and makeshift shrines all around the small enclosed space.

As Jefferson studied the temporary memorial wall, a wire fence encrusted with mementos, flags, messages and even hats left by visitors to the site from all over the world, he tried to imagine what it must have been like to have realized that death was imminent and that thousands might perish if another target were to be reached. To have brought the airplane down in this field, short of Washington DC, was remarkable, and courageous. It was a story of Americans fighting back at the most basic level. It made Jefferson think of another field not so far away to the east. A little place called Gettysburg.

Because it had been forty minutes late leaving the airport, the passengers were able to learn by cell phone that their hijacked airliner was one of four taken by terrorists that day and that the other three planes had hurtled like giant bombs into the World Trade Center's twin towers and into the Pentagon. They had decided to act to prevent a fourth catastrophe. But this temporary memorial site…it wasn't the actual cash site, was it? It had been placed far from the field of death to preserve the sanctity of the hallowed ground, and had originally been closed to the public, only allowing families of the victims to have access. And now the owner of the private property was refusing to renew the lease. It was time for the National Park Service to step in.

An official memorial structure was planned but somehow, Jefferson found the personal offerings, the medallions, and the crosses to be more moving than the design any architect could create. Everywhere there were small monuments: stones engraved with uplifting messages from Boy Scout Troops, public school students, plaques and hand-made flags, painted rocks—the simple and the elaborate. These made the forty victims real and their struggles both horrific and heroic.

Jefferson stepped out through the rail fence and hiked across the field toward where the approximate coordinates of the crash site lay (he had learned this from various web sites that gave the GPS data). It was a distance of about 500 yards. The crash site, obviously, had been cleaned of debris and artifacts. There had been an impact crater nearly fifty feet in diameter and ten feet deep. Small bits of the wreckage had been found up to eight miles away, but the bulk of the aircraft and its terrible cargo were concentrated near the crater. Human remains were collected within a 70 acre radius. There would be, thankfully, nothing to see. But there would be an aura—not of ghosts, not of terror, but of heroism. Jefferson wanted to feel this directly. When the passengers had rushed the cockpit of the hijacked plane they had performed an act of affirmation, giving the cycle of life and death an elevated and noble meaning that would affect and influence many people.

Yes, he could feel it. He could almost hear it.

CAPTAIN JASON DAHL: Mayday! Mayday! Mayday!

CLEVELAND AIR TRAFFIC CONTROLLER: Somebody call Cleveland?

SOMEONE IN THE COCKPIT SHOUTING: Mayday! Mayday! Get out of here! Mayday! Get out of here!

The hijackers assume control of the cockpit and corral the passengers at the rear of the plane. Captain Dahl struggles with the hijackers. Just before he dies, he is able to set the plane on autopilot and switch the output of the cabin microphones to the radio transmitter. The terrorists will now be heard by air traffic controllers.

ZIAD JARRAH, al-Qaeda terrorist, addressing the passengers over the intercom: Ladies and gentlemen: Here the captain. Please sit down, keep remaining seating. We have a bomb on board. So sit.

CLEVELAND AIR TRAFFIC CONTROLLER: Calling Cleveland center, you're unreadable. Say again, slowly.

Debbie Welsh, first-class flight attendant, struggles with the terrorists. She is silenced, probably killed.

JARRAH: Here's the captain: I would like to tell you all to remain seated. We have a bomb aboard, and we are going back to the airport, and we have our demands. So please remain quiet.

Passengers begin making phone calls using their cell phones and the GTE in-flight phones. They learn about the attacks on the World Trade Center and the Pentagon.

TOM BURNETT to his wife: The hijackers...talking about crashing this plane.... Oh my God. It's a suicide mission!

LAUREN GRANDCOLAS to her husband: Jack, pick up sweetie, can you hear me? Okay. I just want to tell you, there's a little problem with the plane. I'm fine. I'm totally fine. I just want to tell you how much I love you.

MARION BRITTON to her friend, Fred Fiumano: We're gonna. They're gonna kill us, you know, We're gonna die.

FRED FIUMANO: Don't worry, they hijacked the plane, they're gonna take you for a ride, you go to their country, and you come back. You stay there for vacation. Be calm.

HONOR ELIZABETH WAINIO to her stepmother: I have to go. They're breaking into the cockpit. I love you.

HIJACKERS IN THE COCKPIT: Is there something? A fight?

JARRAH: They want to get in here. Hold, hold from the inside. Hold from the inside. Hold.... Is that it? Shall we finish it off?

ANOTHER HIJACKER: No. Not yet. When they all come, we finish it off.

A PASSENGER IN THE HALLWAY TO THE COCKPIT: In the cockpit. If we don't, we'll die. Then: Roll it!

The passengers use a food cart as a battering ram to burst open the cockpit door. They breach the door and struggle with the hijackers over control of the airplane. The airplane goes into a nosedive and rolls upside down.

TERRORIST: Allah is the greatest.

The last sound is the shrieking of wind, and then a horrific explosion.

5

The Glass Negatives

This time her feet were in sandals. "I've a surprise for you," she said. She led him back through the house to a small room off the kitchen. What had been a pantry for the original owners of the house had been converted into a powder room. Because it had running water and no windows it was the perfect location for a darkroom. Betty had set up a small table to hold the trays and hung up a safelight that would not expose the light-sensitive paper. "Followed your directions to the letter. Aren't I wonderful?"

In his mind, Jefferson answered, yes. I could kiss you. In his mind she answered, yes, why don't you. But this exchange was not to happen, not yet at any rate. Instead, Jefferson began to explain the techniques of darkroom photography they would use to produce prints from the glass negatives. How they would make test exposures to determine how much time to shine light through the negatives onto the paper to render a good image. How the developing solution would change the exposed silver on the paper to various shades of black. How the fixer would dissolve the unexposed silver. Then washing and drying and the magic would be complete.

They went through the box of plates and selected a few that seemed less deteriorated than the rest. "It's funny, seeing the world in reversed values," she said, referring to the negatives where black was white and white was black. "Sometimes I wonder which state is the normal one," he replied, an obtuse comment no doubt, but revealing of his sometimes dark outlook on life. He tried reversing the mood he had created by saying, "Well, think how useful it would be, for instance, in situations of racial tension, if you could trade black for white and white for black." This elicited a weak giggle from Betty, which he followed with a self-conscious chuckle.

They took the plates to the makeshift darkroom. Jefferson poured chemicals into the trays: developer, short stop, and fixer. There was a fourth tray in the sink with water running into it. He measured temperatures, and declared they were ready for a test strip. Off with the room light, on with the safelight. Paper with sensitive side facing up, glass plate with emulsion side down in contact with the paper. A piece of cardboard placed to allow a fraction of the plate/paper sandwich to be exposed by light. Room lights on for one second (a low-wattage bulb replaced the normal one). Pull the cardboard back, lights again, repeat until a serious of progressively longer exposures had been made on the single sheet of photo paper. Into the developer. Timed. Short stop solution to stop the development. Fixer. Wait. Room lights again and evaluate.

"Looks like about three seconds will give us a good rendering of black to white with grays in the right places."

"This is really exciting," she replied.

"Now we do a good print."

They stood together, their bodies touching slightly, as the first image began to form in the tray. There was something about the way in which the picture began to appear; at first, the darkest shadows materializing as light gray tones, then darkening as the middle tones emerged, and then the whole image slowly solidifying into a recognizable scene, floating just beneath the surface of the developer. Tinted yellow-orange by the safelight, the slow birthing of the image of a face or a landscape seemed like some alchemist's slight of hand. It never failed to amaze. Betty was delighted. "Let me do the next one," she said.

They had tested and printed a half-dozen of the glass negatives. The prints hung from clips on a wire to dry while Betty and Jefferson relaxed in the living room, feeling proud and exhilarated. They traded stories and Jefferson marveled at the openness they each exhibited. She told him about growing up in the village, feeling stifled and wanting desperately to escape.

"Did you ever get away?"

"Penn State. Wasn't all I expected, though. But I did meet my husband there."

"You're married?"

"He was killed in Afghanistan."

"I'm so sorry."

"We'd only been married a year when it happened. He stepped on a mine and was killed instantly. I'm over it now," Betty said. Jefferson thought her voice trembled a little.

"I inherited some money and this house from an aunt and moved back a couple years ago. I've been focused on this History Museum since then. And you?"

"Divorced. Her name was Joyce. We were high school sweethearts. The old story, I suppose. Hot romance that fizzled. She said I was too demanding, jealous and controlling."

"Were you?"

"I don't remember it that way. Joyce said I was harboring unresolved issues from some unrequited adolescent love affair. She was the suspicious one."

"You sound like the perfect couple, both jealous and self-possessed." Did Jefferson look hurt by this observation? She tried to recoup. "Oh, I'm sorry! That wasn't called for. It's just that, well, I know what you mean."

"Your husband and you..."

She nodded. Sitting on the davenport across from him she could see the tension in his body language. Were they getting a little too personal?

"That was part of the shock of losing him," she explained. "We never got to work things out."

"Perhaps you would have. I'd hope so, anyway."

"That's kind of you." (Now change the subject.) "So, why the interest in cemetery photography?"

"I don't know. I guess I get along better with dead people than live ones. Trying to understand and reconstruct the past is fascinating. And there is something about the serenity of a cemetery. The older ones are the most peaceful."

"Don't you find them sad?"

"I find them eternal."

When the prints were dry they spread them on the dining room table and surveyed them. They were mostly portraits, taken in a studio, the sitters straight-backed against painted backgrounds. The clothing and hair styles evoked another era, one of pride and self reliance and strict adherence to propriety. Perhaps it was sitting still for the long exposures used at that time that made their expressions seem otherworldly, even possessed. Like dreamers caught in time that had stopped, unable to advance or retreat as the rest of the universe unraveled around them. But now, thought Jefferson, they were saved. Frozen, but safe and eternal in a photograph, an eternity more appealing than that of the grave.

Was his Elizabeth there in one of those pictures? No, he realized, glass plates hadn't been used during her lifetime. Perhaps his namesake? Maybe. There was a photograph of a young man dressed in a Civil War army uniform. He sported great mutton chop sideburns and attempted a smile that read as a smirk, cocksure in his pose as he brandished a rifle in the position of "present arms." At his side hung a saber with a bit of tassel that seemed too decorative, too ceremonial for the role he would play in the acts which would follow.

"Is there any way to learn who these people were?" Jefferson asked. Betty was the expert, wasn't she? There would be records of some kind, wouldn't there?

"The box was found in the attic of an old house that was going to be torn down. I can look up the records for the owners. Maybe the man was a photographer. Why else would there have been so many portraits?"

"There would have been a photography studio in town. Would they have kept records?"

"We are just beginning to sort through the relics of our historical past here. It was mostly a mining town…a company town. The records that were kept didn't often reflect the lives of the people who did the work…just the dollars and cents of it."

Jefferson shuffled through the prints and retrieved the Civil War soldier. "This one," he said. "How could I find out more about him?"

"The National Archives has many records of the American Civil War. You can go online and search their data base."

Of course, he thought to himself. I am stupid. Research on the internet! He gave her a broad smile.

"Where are you staying tonight?" she asked.

"I didn't check out of the motel in Somerset. Left my things there."

"You could stay here…I've plenty of room. Just until we're done with the prints."

"Thanks, but the motel has free wifi. I can get a lot of research done there tonight."

"I've got a computer. Say, I'd invite you to stay for dinner, but…ah…I don't cook."

"We could order a pizza."

And so the mini-romance of Betty and Jefferson proceeded, snail-like but turtle-sure. He would return to the motel that night. He would spend hours pouring through something called "The Index to Compiled Service Records of Volunteer Union Soldiers from Pennsylvania," and "The Compiled Military Service Records (CMSR)," and "The Descriptive List of Drafted Men, with Exemptions." and pension records, and census records, and many an index to the microfilm collections held by The National Archives and Records Administration (NARA).

But he was finding that even in this day and age of computers and internet web sites, a great percentage of the records existing from the last two centuries were stored as musty, dusty, hand-written papers, bound in volumes or loose in archival boxes, shelved in a diverse and scattered number of libraries and historical society buildings, and that only a fraction of these had even been microfilmed, much less digitized and ported to a searchable database.

He would sleep and perhaps dream, and the dreams that would come would be peopled with uniforms of blue and of gray—and of red—crimson and scarlet stuff that dripped and stained—and of other foul colors and odors and sounds. Flashes in the night sky, smoke that blocked the morning sun, the rattle of grapeshot against trees and wagons and horses and men. And the wails of the wounded, the yip of the Rebel yell, the canon's belch of ball, or bits of chain and metal; resounding and echoing and never quite leaving the ear but persisting as a dull ringing long after the battle had subsided. His sleep would be troubled by these imagined images.

Byron Grush

6

Cemetery Hill

There was a cemetery up on the top of the hill. He was crouched against a stone wall on the northern slope, cleaning mud from his boots and listening to the sound of musket fire in the distance. It was a hot July afternoon and bluebottle flies buzzed around his head. For some reason, the Rebel troops had held off attacking his position giving him and his fellow soldiers a brief respite. They knew to take advantage of the interlude while there was only an occasional artillery shell to harass them.

His company, the 75th Pennsylvania, was deployed along the wall and out into the lane. Some sprawled smoking, gnawing on hardtack or laughing at each other's jokes. The man next to him gestured with a plug of chewing tobacco but he shook his head. The light began to fade and a silent tension permeated the scene as if nature herself had held her breath while the day departed.

The attack began with a chorus of rebel yells, a shrill screeching and hooting that was a cross between an Indian war whoop and the barking of wild dogs hot on the trail of a fox or a hog. They used to say if you weren't frightened by a rebel yell then you probably hadn't ever heard one. In the semidarkness, men shuffled around for greater cover but the musket balls came too close to allow much movement. He saw one of his company lurch suddenly, a dark red spot forming against the blue of his uniform. Above them, on Cemetery Hill, the Union artillery boomed, flashes illuminating clouds in the evening sky; thunder and lightning for the terrible storm of battle.

At a weak point in the Union defenses, the gray clad Confederate troops were able to breach the wall and came pouring over it in a flood of destruction. Man clashed with man in personal combat, bayonet, sword or knife swinging furiously. He thrust his bayonet into the chest of a man as he vaulted the wall. The man seemed not to die but to continue walking toward him like some senseless zombie. He squeezed the trigger of his rifle and the man was carried away off the bayonet in a haze of redness by the impact. All around him was chaos.

Up on the ridge the artillery had difficulty directing their hell-fire against the enemy: the hill was too steep to allow angling the barrels properly. Mortar and canister were of little use, not being accurate and often sending missiles astray or into friendly troops. On the southern slope, on Raffensperger's Hill, sat the old Evergreen Cemetery. The Union commanders were squirreled into the small gatehouse there, using it as a headquarters. Word came that the Confederate forces, North Carolinians and Louisianians, had breeched the stone wall and were headed for the batteries on the top of the hill. The fools were fighting in the dark!

The 58th and the 119th New York brigades were diverted from West Cemetery Hill to engage the Confederate assault on the artillery batteries; another brigade from Cemetery Ridge was also deployed. The Rebels would soon be routed, pushed back down the hill. What could have been a decisive victory for the South, had it been coordinated properly, would be a disaster—both sides incurring heavy losses, neither gaining an advantage. There would be medals for the dead and the dying. Advancements for the officers. Coffins for the widows to bury.

He was in the thick of it. The press of bodies was interminable. His rifle was of no use except as a bludgeon. He swung out with his bowie knife, turning in circles, slashing at the throats of young men and boys he might otherwise have called friend, brother, cousin, father. What noble cause was this? To stay alive. To last out the darkness, the horror, the desperation. To return home, not missing an arm or a leg, an eye, or a part of a face. To be victorious—what did *that* mean?

He could hear the reinforcements arriving to turn the tide: the triumphant shouting, the muffled reports of musket fire, the clatter of swords and bayonets, the unique, unforgettable, ugly utterance of men struck by grapeshot or gored by pike…a kind of wheeze and bellow and shriek combined, as if voice were propelled by the flight of the soul from the body. He could hear that, all too well.

In the aftermath, the slopes of Cemetery Hill and the nearby fields were dotted with the dead and the dying, blue, gray and red in the grass and dirt. Bodies and parts of bodies glistened in the morning light as turkey vultures circled patiently overhead. He lay among them, a musket ball lodged in his chest, his life's blood spreading out in an ever-expanding pool. His vision blurred and his breath came in shorter and shorter gasps. As he began to drift toward a welcomed unconsciousness, he thought of her.

Her skin was damp and sticky. Kissing her neck left him with a salty taste. He had been apprehensive when she led him to the bedroom. He had turned away while undressing, an action which caused her to laugh. When she pulled him onto the comforter, tittering like a little girl, probing and tickling him, his fears left him and he rolled on top of her. They embraced passionately at first, then a quiet, relaxed exploration began. "Here," she said. "And here." As she became more explicit in her directions he became withdrawn. He didn't like talking during sex. He could feel his enthusiasm becoming languid. "Don't stop," she said. "Stop talking," he said. "Tell me what you want," she said. "Ssssh!" he said. "Maybe if I play dead?" she said.

(Was it years ago? It seemed so.) He had traveled to Philadelphia, a distance of over 230 miles, walking most of the way. There was a man there, a Colonel Henry Bohlen, who was organizing a volunteer infantry regiment to fight in the great conflict for the preservation of the Union. He wanted to fight. He volunteered, was accepted for duty, and soon found himself fitting out at Camp Worth just west of the city. Found himself marching through the streets of Philadelphia, proudly parading and prepared to enter the fray. Found himself on a troop train, headed for Washington. Found himself crossing the Potomac, then camped in Virginia, waiting…waiting for a proper battle.

There had been a draft, the so-called Enrollment Act, passed by the Thirty-seventh Congress, which was intended to swell the ranks of the Union Army. But he couldn't wait to be drafted. And he had nothing but distain for the wealthy and the elite who took advantage of a provision in the Act that allowed them to pay $300 for a substitute to serve for them. (Some very prominent men, young and in good health, had never served; among them were future U.S. President Glover Cleveland and the rich and famous John D. Rockefeller.)

They were to ferry across the Shenandoah River, to pursue General Stonewall Jackson. Ice floats clogged the river and made navigating with the rafts hazardous. The river rushed with a contentious fury. There was an old ferry boat but the enemy had set fire to it. Companies K and I repaired this, and guided by a rope stretched across the river, they set out into the raging current. But the boat began to sink at midstream. Fifty men met death in that icy torrent. This was his first encounter with the horrors of war. Men died…but there was supposed to be valor and honor, not senseless waste. He would soon get to experience the valor and honor of righteous engagement. And death by the wagonload.

They nearly starved during the long march to the Shenandoah Valley. Near Harrisburg, Virginia, at the Battle of Cross Keys, they finally saw action. At first held in reserve, they began to advance to relieve other units. The enemy was entrenched along creek and river, in woods and on hilltop. The Union generals had sought to outflank but had miscalculated the enemy positions. In the skirmishes there was a great loss of life on the Union side. To make way for artillery fire a retreat was called. In the aftermath they learned that the Confederate Army had abandoned its position. As they buried the dead, they were informed that this had been a Confederate victory…a hollow one.

At the Battle of Rappahannock Station at Freeman's Ford, the 75th's commander, now Brigadier General Bohlen, was killed by musket fire during the initial attack. Union forces were pinned down allowing Stonewall Jackson to march through Thoroughfare Gap to capture Bristoe Station and destroy Federal supplies at Manassas Junction. Next the 75th marched toward Manassas. But at Groveton they encountered both the forces of General Ewell and General Jackson, among the fiercest of the Confederate South. Again there was great loss of life. The 75th Pennsylvania fought bravely and they were commended by their superiors. Across Bull Run and on to Centreville they fought. And now the Second Battle of Manassas was deemed a Confederate victory…this one not so hollow.

Then came Chancellorsville. The Union army, under the command of Major General Joseph Hooker stood against General Robert E. Lee's North Virginians—an army of half the size of Hooker's Army of the Potomac. It would be the second bloodiest battle of the war, and would stand throughout history as a shining example of General Lee's brilliance. Lee out-flanked and routed Hooker who had made several tactical errors. Although Lieutenant General Stonewall Jackson was mortally wounded during the fray, this was a decisive Confederate victory and one that further demoralized the Union Army. The 75th found themselves scattered among other regiments near the Wilderness Church at Chancellorsville.

And then came Gettysburg. Colonel Mahler, who had taken over command of the regiment after General Bohlen had his horse shot out from under him. He was wounded and subsequently died from his wounds. Captain Saalmann of Company C, taking command, was also critically wounded. The next leader, Lieutenant Sill received a bullet wound in his leg; his leg was amputated; he also died from his wounds. Major August Ledig then took command, positioning the 75th Pennsylvania at Cemetery Hill. And then the Rebels breached the wall and stormed the artillery battery—and our soldier, who had survived all of this, lay dying.

During the Battle of Gettysburg, the 75th Pennsylvania suffered 31 dead, nearly 72 percent of its officers and enlisted men. 100 were wounded and 6 were taken prisoner. He was lucky to be alive. Now he lay in a tent on a blood-stained cot; all around him were wounded and dying men, Outside the tent was a gruesome pile of severed limbs and blood-soaked rags. The tent served as a makeshift hospital until the wounded could be conveyed to better facilities—only there weren't any better facilities.

"How you doin' private?" the medic asked him. He stared up at the man who seemed to be covered with more blood then he was. Wasn't the medic's blood though, was it?

Screams came from the rear of the tent where an amputation was taking place. *Lord, take me back to the battlefield*, he thought to himself. "How *am* I doing?" he responded to the medic.

"You'll be fine, You've lost a lot of blood, but we've stopped the bleeding. Now just pray you avoid infection. You're lucky, You'll be going home, son."

7

The Celebration

"I think I may have found your soldier," Betty told Jefferson when he arrived the next morning to continue printing from the glass plates. "Only Jefferson isn't his first name...it's his surname."

Jefferson was intrigued. He hadn't expected to be able to track down "his soldier" so quickly. Of course, he had been searching on "Jefferson" as a first name.

"Look what I found in the archives. A newspaper article from 1913. It seems there was to be a reunion of the veterans of the battles at Gettysburg as part of its fiftieth anniversary."

Jefferson looked at the copy she had made of the newspaper. Funny, how the type was so small and crude-looking. And advertisements were peppered throughout the page with no apparent order—probably to fill space as necessary, he thought. He read the headline: "Local War Heroes to Attend Celebration."

The Pennsylvania Assembly had created a Fiftieth Anniversary of the Battle of Gettysburg Commission. Said commission had planned programs to take place on the historic battlefield including a Peace Jubilee during which they would set the cornerstone for a Great Peace Memorial. All honorably discharged veterans from the Grand Army of the Republic and the United Confederate Veterans were invited to take place in an encampment. President Woodrow Wilson would address the participants. There were concerns, of course that there might be "unpleasant differences" between the two groups of veterans.

Among the "Local Heroes" was one Silas Jefferson, a former private in the 75th Pennsylvania, who had been wounded at Gettysburg.

"Do you think this is the same man we have in the picture?" Jefferson asked.

"There is no way to tell that at this point. I looked for more articles, hoping for pictures of the group from Somerset County but I haven't found anything yet. Look at this, though. Remember the comment about unpleasant differences? Read this article in the Pittsburg Press from July 1, 1913."

He read:

Pathetic Night Scene in Veterans' Great Reunion

Yesterday afternoon the dedication of the Lee uncompleted [Virginia] monument took place. NOTE: A violent event away from the reunion was at Hotel Gettysburg where a man used a "vile epithet" for President Lincoln and stabbed 8 people. The VA governor subsequently spoke on behalf of the perpetrator. A Philadelphia attorney in the area is to locate his father that he claimed was a Confederate general. The father, a Confederate Major posted the bail.

"But just one lunatic who probably had too much to drink? The celebration was otherwise peaceful, I take it. I wonder how many veterans came to Gettysburg for those days."

"I think they planned for twelve to thirteen thousand. But there might have been more. Can you picture it: the vast battlefield covered with thousands of tents; old men with long, unruly beards wearing wool uniforms of blue or gray in the heat of July (it reached 100 degrees); a troop of the very first Boy Scouts serving fried chicken to the veterans; the enactment..."

"There was an enactment?"

"The Confederate veterans walked along the path of Pickett's Charge and were met by Union veterans with whom they shook hands."

"There is something ironic and sad about that. As if a celebration of presumed bravery and loyalty could negate the brutal reality of a stupid and tragic conflict…a war I believe we are still fighting!"

"You're a bit cynical, aren't you?" Betty said, half taunting Jefferson.

"Well, you know what they say: 'cynicism is the spice of life.' "

"That's from some movie, isn't it? *Fargo* or something?"

"You're thinking of 'sarcasm is the spice of life,' a sort of cliché based on 'variety is the spice of life.' Also, it is in another movie, *Malice*, where the sheriff says '…it's just that kind of sarcasm that's given our marriage real spice.' So you could say, 'sarcasm is the spice of our marriage.' Or something like that."

"Sarcasm, cynicism…what's the point?"

"I think it was Lillian Hellman who said 'cynicism is an unpleasant way of saying the truth.' I don't know how we got onto this, but I do have some strong beliefs about the futility of war."

"I can see that," Betty said. "What did Shakespeare have to say about it?"

"Old Bill said, and I quote, 'your lips are like wine and I want to get drunk.' "

"I hope you're not just being sarcastic."

It was different, very different from the intimacy he and Joyce had…shared? No, not shared, because he and Joyce had never really experienced things in the same way. Joyce had accommodated him in sex, giving an expert, feigned performance of enthralled ecstasy that had he accepted naively, and without regard for *her* needs. It had been a classic delusional relationship, a non-correspondence that neither had acknowledged nor attempted to repair. And then it was too late.

This was different, very different. This was a first-blush-on-the-rose sort of encounter for Jefferson; as if he and Betty were the first humans on earth, discovering why the Deity (did he believe in one? —it didn't really matter) had made them opposite and compatible. It was as if the habits of adulthood and marriage had been erased, psyches made blank, and, through cautious exploration, their senses had led them to an ecstatic revelation. His desire had been tempered with gentle creativity. There were secrets to be unearthed with care. There were tastes and smells and tactile perceptions to be detected, slowly savored, generously given.

For Betty it was the long desired fulfillment of a passion she had known only briefly, and clumsily. She had mourned its loss as she had mourned her husband, Brian. It was difficult at first to surrender to her desires—not that there was heartfelt guilt or fear of intimacy—it was only that she had grown accustomed to that hollow part of her, that empty, aching disablement that had attached like a parasite to her every activity, her every striving, and had held her in a kind of limbo from which she had seen no possible escape. Now Jefferson had come into her life and awakened that other part—the part she had held in check in deference to Brian. The part that belonged to a ghost. The part that was the sexual essence of Betty Snyder.

For the rest of the day they lay on the bed, sheets and blankets tossed onto the floor, pillows in disarray, the cat prowling rudely between entwined limbs. A soft breeze blew the lace curtains and faint noises of the life outside of their sphere of mutual seduction wafted through the open windows: a bus noisily exhaling its noxious exhaust, an errant motorcycle revving and sputtering, a distant lawnmower growling through grass too thick to cut easily, a lonesome dog wailing, children laughing, airliners whistling, angry crows cackling. A symphony of the ordinary accompanied the sounds of breathing (not heavy), and cooing (not *too* silly), and quiet words whispered (only the cat could hear), and the resumption of clutching, rolling, thrusting, grunting (which sounds are omitted here…as propriety prescribes).

Morning became afternoon; afternoon became early evening. Stomachs growled. Food was required. Betty and Jefferson rose, dressed, and wandered out and along the avenue that led into a district where fast food restaurants lurked on every corner, each sporting backlit signs touting two-for-one specials and super-sized fries, shakes, cokes and burgers.

"Ugh," said Jefferson.

"We'll go to Margie's," said Betty. "Good old homestyle cookin' and actual table cloths. Just down the block, next to Starbucks."

Red and white checkered table cloths made of cotton—not plastic. Water glasses with ice and a slice of lemon. A short glass vase with a freshly picked sprig of lily of the valley. A basket of fresh, warm rolls. A type-written menu slightly stained with spots that might have been gravy. A stout waitress, her hair pinned up, smiling and asking, "How are we today?" Jefferson was in his element.

"I don't suppose you're still serving breakfast. Are you?"

Jefferson wanted to know.

"Sorry, Hun. Special today's chicken-fried steak and tater-tots, early June peas and apple sauce. Soup is French onion with grated cheese. Can I get ya started with the relish tray? Help yourself to three bean salad, cheese dip for the veggies, pickled herring…just don't spoil yer appetites!"

Jefferson and Betty both ordered meatloaf with garlic mashed potatoes. They repaired to the relish tray table and heaped small plates with olives, pickled beets, Ritz crackers, carrot and celery sticks, cherry tomatoes and pickled gherkins. After returning to their table, Betty asked, "So what happens now?"

"What do you mean?"

"I mean, are you staying, going…what are your plans? I know I invited you to stay at my house, but…"

"But the neighbors might talk. Yes, I thought of that. Small town, big gossip. That's one reason I didn't park my car in your driveway."

"Expecting a quick getaway? That was the other reason?"

"No, Betty. I…I haven't been with anyone in a while. And I didn't expect…I didn't think we would…"

"But we did. The glass plates will all be printed after tomorrow. You're free to go romping around the country, documenting your dead people."

"I'm in no hurry. I could stay a few more days. Help you frame the prints. That is, if you'd like some help."

Betty plucked an anchovy-stuffed olive from her small plate and held it momentarily between her lips before sucking it into her mouth. Her eyes told him the answer to his question.

"Isn't there an old hotel in town? I could stay there," he suggested.

"You mean the Grand Midway? It was built in the late 1890s. It started out as a brothel for the local miners. There are stories of murders and unnatural deaths taking place there…it's supposed to be haunted."

"Haunted? Sounds like the place for me!"

"Well, it's a private residence now. Somebody bought it on Ebay several years ago. I think they open up the bar now and then and have music and art shows…I guess you could ask to stay there. If you weren't afraid of the ghosts, of course."

"What kind of ghosts could there possibly be in a quaint little town like this one?"

"There is a small female child supposedly buried in the basement. And there's the Professor, who is seen walking around holding a book. Ghosts are seen sitting at the windows at night and there are unexplainable shadows on the walls. There are underground tunnels beneath the house and an attic that is sealed up…"

"Every town has an old house that people say is haunted. Is there any real evidence of strange deaths?"

"I have an old newspaper article from, I think, 1911, about a young woman who was killed in a bizarre way. Her name was Martha Minnie Cerwinsky or Selinsky. She was 17 or 18 and was watching from the second floor balcony of the hotel as the Windber Fire Company was setting off fireworks up on Graham Avenue. They would use iron pipes to hold the rockets as they lit them. But one misfired and the pipe exploded, sending bits of metal flying. A piece of metal struck Martha in the neck and ripped out her throat. She bled to death. One account states that her blood dripped off the porch onto a baby carriage on the sidewalk below."

"Gruesome! And I bet people can see her ghost walking the balcony."

"Hers is probably the strongest presence at the Grand Midway. You don't believe in ghosts, do you? You hang around cemeteries a lot. Ever seen any ghosts?"

"Not on my watch. And I don't believe there are spirit manifestations like the Spiritualists pretend to evoke…ectoplasm and all that. However, there are certain places where you can definitely feel a presence. The Grandview Cemetery in Westmont, for instance. There is a burial plot there for 777 of the unidentified victims of the Johnstown flood of 1889. When you stand by that, you sense…something. Some connection to…well…not an afterlife, but an essence…an energy, like the residue of a life force that lingers because it has no place else to go."

They were interrupted by the waitress bringing their meatloaf and mashed potatoes. "Watch out, these are hot," she said. Then she gestured toward the small plates. "Still workin'?" she asked.

8

The Professor's Ghost

They had printed a little over two dozen of the glass negatives. Not all of the resulting images had been rewarding since a fair percentage of the plates had deteriorated. Jefferson actually liked the way the flaked edges of emulsion produced a sort of vignette, but he had to agree that sometimes cracks and bubbles interfered with any possibility of identifying the subjects of the photographs.

The bulk of them were from the mysterious photographer's studio which Betty had been unable to find listed in any of the city directories. She surmised the studio had most likely been located in Somerset or Johnstown, or possibly even in Pittsburg. The photographer, she believed, had "retired" to Windber and brought the box of glass plates with him. Or, just as likely, some collector of antiquities had found the box in a resale shop and stored it away in their attic. The house in which the plates had been found had been standing empty for many years, then had been torn down to make way for a parking lot; there was no record of the property's previous owners.

Photographic prints were spread out across Betty's dining room table. They were to select some for framing. Betty opened the heavy drapes to obtain more light when just at that same moment the cat leaped onto the table, scattering photographs in every direction.

"Bartholomew! You naughty cat. Get down from there!" she yelled.

Jefferson bent to pick up some of the prints that had fallen on the floor. One in particular caught his eye. "Say, look at this. I hadn't noticed this one before."

The print was of a man with a heavy dark beard seated in an ornate upholstered chair with carved arms that swirled into a kind of curlicue resembling a question mark. He was sparse of hair on top of his head which gave his elongated face an imbalance and accented dark, brooding eyes that peered from under his shadowed brows. One elbow rested on an arm of the chair while the other held a book on his lap. The book was clearly rendered by the sharp focus of the camera lens and Jefferson could see that it had an elegant binding, most likely leather with gold embossed designs. The man's suit jacket was open at the bottom and a watch chain dangled from a vest pocket. Next to this tableau of the portrait sitter was a low table covered with a decorated cloth and behind that...

"There is a figure of some kind here. At first I though it was an anomaly caused by deterioration or by uneven development or just by a stain. But it resembles..."

In the space just above the table in the photograph there appeared the pale, ghostly image of a robed man wearing a turban. His arm was stretched out toward the seated man and he seemed to be offering a sheet of paper or document. It was faint, but there was too much detail for it to be a stain or the effect of bad developing.

"Oh my God!" said Betty. "I think we found the Professor."

The "Professor" was one of the ghosts often seen at the haunted Grand Midway Hotel. But if the man in the portrait was the Professor, he was clearly not the ghost in this picture. Had anyone ever seen the ghost of a man wearing a turban?

"You know what...it's trick photography," said Jefferson. "In the nineteenth century there were photographers who produced things like this to aid the cause of Spiritualism, or just to make money, I suppose. It's probably a double exposure to create the effect of a translucent figure. Notice how well the scene is composed to allow just enough space for the 'ghost' to appear next to the man?"

"I suppose you're right. But it makes a good story, doesn't it?"

Jefferson went to the box where the glass plates were stored, now neatly tucked into archival paper envelopes. He found the one with the bearded man and slid it from its envelope. He held it up against the light coming through the window.

"That's odd," he said. "I can't see any darker area where the 'ghost' should be on this plate. It's just not there!"

Jefferson spent the following day walking another cemetery on the outskirts of Windber. It was called the Oldham Graveyard or more commonly, the Crum Cemetery, and it was, to Jefferson's consternation and annoyance, haunted. Or at least that was what was said about the old abandoned hill top cemetery where nearly 60 headstones of various ages and conditions sat upright or leaning on the well-kept grounds. Jefferson was annoyed by this urban lore of ghostly sightings because it attracted the morbidly curious, the teenaged thrill seekers, and the senseless vandals to the site. And it was the second time in only a few days that supernatural manifestations were to impose upon his otherwise professional (and recreational) activities.

It was, indeed, maintained—but by whom? There was no town, not anymore. The small village of Crum now consisted of a decrepit hunting cabin, the remains of a few crumbling stone foundations, and this cemetery. It was another of those mid-nineteenth century towns where immigrant families had worked at logging—until the forests had given out and the population had dwindled to practically nothing. Then Big Coal had come along with offers to buy which the remaining residents could not refuse. No coal was mined here, however, so no new jobs were available; the company wanted the land in order to control the watershed and supply drinking water to its own company towns where they had recklessly polluted their own water. The town was now deserted—a ghost town, with a real ghost.

And the haunting? Jefferson had looked it up on the internet. The most popular ghost story was related to a woman named Rebecca Crum. She had been known around the old town for selling herbal remedies and apparently had been versed in Native American healing arts and rituals. This, of course, had led to accusations of witchcraft. She was either buried alive in an unmarked grave or burned alive along with her family in their home, or burned along with the entire village after cursing it with a devastating plague. Rebecca was a very vocal ghost and her wails and cries could be heard throughout the surrounding woods. Some said one could see the wispy form of a lady dressed in white floating through the air. Others claimed to have seen a black horse-drawn carriage rumbling around the grounds at night.

There is, however, no record of a Rebecca Crum. Nor of a fire, nor of a plague. There was another Rebecca, a Rebecca Kring, who supposedly haunted another Western Pennsylvania cemetery, the Snavely Cemetery near Elton (commonly known as Becky's Grave). Becky was supposedly a witch who was hung for practicing black magic, or she was killed along with her husband in a fire (set by the villagers?) that consumed their home. She was 83. She is actually buried in a different cemetery than the one where her ghost is reportedly seen lurking at night. It was funny, thought Jefferson, how these stories were so similar—and so ludicrous. At both locations, it was said, cars would refuse to start. A good excuse for teenage necking?

Jefferson moved from marker to marker, taking photographs, writing details from the stones in his notebook. Often the inscriptions were so weather worn they were impossible to decipher. On sunny days like this one, the fronts of some stones would be in deep shadow, or angled so that harsh sunlight caused reflections that ruined the image. Jefferson had large pieces of cardboard in the Subaru which he used to control the natural lighting. Today was overcast, dull and shadowless. Perfect for his purposes.

He set up the camera on the tripod for a long shot; an overall picture to show the lay of the land, so to speak. The camera had a state of the art LCD screen and as Jefferson focused, a white blotch appeared behind one of the larger monuments. He looked up but there was nothing there. A lens flare? But it wasn't sunny. He cleaned the lens using a soft cloth and lens cleaning fluid. Then he cleaned the LCD screen. But the blotch or flare or whatever it was, was still there. Oh crap, he thought. The screen is going out. I can work around it, but it might mean purchasing a new camera. He snapped the picture and loaded his gear into the Subaru, thinking about stopping back at Betty's before returning to his motel (he hadn't moved in with the girl—he wasn't ready to commit to that—yet).

Betty had made spaghetti. She had cut thin slices of French bread which she had buttered and sprinkled with garlic salt, then placed under the broiler for several minutes. She had constructed a tossed salad with lettuce, green peppers, tomatoes and cucumbers. She had found a bottle of merlot tucked away in a cupboard. Jefferson had opened this with a flourish of expertise that was, perhaps, overly dramatic, offering Betty the cork to sniff (she simply tossed this into the trash can).

"See," Jefferson said, "you *can* cook."

"Yeah, I can boil water, dump store-bought pasta into it, and open a jar of sauce."

"It takes skill to open a jar of sauce."

After they finished washing the dishes (Jefferson dried) Betty said, "Stay tonight. I feel lonely when you go to that motel."

"What about the neighbors?"

"The neighbors will be envious. Anyway, who cares?"

"I care. But I'll stay. I want to get going early in the morning, though. I want to get to another site."

"You and your dead friends!"

Jefferson walked from the kitchen and picked up his laptop which he had left on a hall table.

"I'm going to work for a little while…transferring the pictures I shot today to my laptop to make room on the camera."

"Well, don't be long. I have plans for you."

Jefferson attached a cable between his camera and his laptop and began transferring photos. He examined the camera, and failed to find the mysterious blotch on the viewing screen. Strange. Perhaps it had been some sort of magnetic interference when he was at the cemetery. But from what? When the transfer was complete he scrolled through thumb nails of the image files. He found the final picture he had taken, the overview of the cemetery. He clicked on it, enlarging it to full screen. There, near the center of the picture, just behind a large monument, was the blotch. Only it wasn't botch-like in the picture. It was the finely detailed image of a man—a man wearing what appeared to be a turban on his head and a long, flowing white robe. The same man Jefferson had found on the print from the glass plate. And just like the man in the glass plate print, he was holding a sheet of paper in his outstretched hand.

Byron Grush

9

The Road Trip

Jefferson had tossed off the blankets sometime in the middle of the night. Now they were twisted around his feet causing him to dream that he was tied and hanging upside down by his legs. He woke with a start. A waking dream is more startling to us than one of deeper sleep because we bring it with us into our so-called real world. It stays with us, a nagging, half remembered sensation, then, once we are fully awake and excited to relate our bizarre dream experience to someone else, it dissipates and refuses to rematerialize. Stubborn dream. Insolent dream. Elusive dream. And so it takes on more meaning than it probably has. We make connections between those elusive snippets and whatever deeply seated anxieties or regrets we harbor. Arrogant dream. Meaningless dream.

"Scary dream," said Jefferson as Betty poured him a cup of hot, aromatic coffee. "Hate that."

"Dreams are supposed to be the mind taking out the garbage," Betty replied, reluctant to sympathize. "They don't mean anything."

"I was a Civil War soldier and I'd been captured by the enemy. They hung me upside down by my feet. I tried to cry out but I couldn't make a sound."

"Then you woke up and found yourself trying to swallow the pillow." Betty nibbled the corner off her piece of toast. "I thought you were in a hurry to get out of here. Miles to go and promises to keep and all that."

"I was. But there's something I'd like to talk over with you." His hand reached out to touch hers. Just before fingers met fingers, he drew it back. He forced a smile which Betty found puzzling.

"Let's take our second cups of coffee out on the front porch," she said. "Fresh air stimulates the mind."

There was an old porch glider at one end of the porch next to an ancient and overgrown magnolia tree which leaned toward the house and created a kind of private space. As they sat, moving the swing ever so slightly with their feet, they could gaze out through the branches and watch people, oblivious to their presence, walking up and down the sidewalk. People watching was something Jefferson did at airports or bus terminals to kill time. He enjoyed fantasizing about strangers: what they did for a living, if their families were well adjusted or dysfunctional, which ones were terrorists with bombs in their shoes...

"You probably know all these people," he observed.

"Some of them...not personally, but I see them around. It's a nice neighborhood. Children play in the streets, dogs run freely...nobody worries too much about crime. Of course, we all watch television. Hear the news about school shootings. Columbine, that one in New Orleans, that horrible shooting at the Amish school in West Nickel Mines...right here in Pennsylvania!"

"I try to avoid politics. Try not to dwell on issues or to characterize the world as being made up of 'us and them.' But I think the mood of the country has suffered during the last eight years with that asshole in the White House. It's okay to be stupid. It's okay to be a bully. It's okay to ignore the consequences of your actions. I can't believe Bush was elected twice!"

"He stole the first election, remember? The Supreme Court basically appointed him president. And if it hadn't been for 9/11, things might be different now."

"If it hadn't been for Bush, we might not have had 9/11. Well, don't get me started."

Betty stopped the gentle motion of the glider with her foot and slid a little closer to Jefferson. "What did you want to talk to me about?" she asked.

"You'll think me crazy. I don't know, I guess it's a matter of perception. We see what we want...or don't want...to see. Perception is never rational. We connect the dots to find patterns that are familiar or desired or feared. We inherited that from the cave man."

"Just what are you trying to tell me?"

"I think I may have a ghost."

The Subaru Forester was 8 years old. It had 160 thousand miles on the odometer, a set of fairly new tires, a not-so-state-of-the-art CD deck, and was probably good for another 160 thousand miles. Jefferson could put the back sets down and sleep in a relatively comfortable fetal position if he had to, which sometimes he had to, and so he always traveled with sleeping bag and camp stove, a water filtration device, candles, and duct tape. The duct tape was the most important item on that list.

He slipped a CD of the "Best of Dire Straits" into the deck. Betty grinned when "Sultans of Swing" began to play. "One of my favorite groups," she said.

"That's a good thing," said Jefferson. "I only have three albums and two of them are Dire Straits."

This morning at breakfast, Jefferson had told Betty Snyder about discovering first, that the image of the "ghost" had disappeared from the glass negative, and second, that it had appeared on his final shot of the day, in his digital camera. They immediately inspected the glass plates again: no ghosts, as Jefferson had said. Then they looked at the print—nothing.

"I am sure I saw the same thing you did," Betty said, completely mystified as now, on neither the plate nor the print, was there any indication that a ghostly image had ever appeared. And of course, when they pulled up Jefferson's final shot on his laptop, there wasn't so much as a speck of dust or a lens flare, much less the figure of a tall man dressed in white wearing a turban and carrying a piece of paper in his outstretched hand.

Jefferson was intent on putting as much distance as he could between himself and this region of paranormal phenomena called Windber, regardless of the disappearance of the turban man. He didn't so much as say this, but he did suggest to Betty that a nice drive through the countryside would clear their heads. In fact, why didn't she come with him on his trek throughout the state in search of graveyards? How romantic was that? It took some persuasion on Jefferson' part and it was only after Betty ascertained that her friend and co-worker at the History Museum, Sally Pleasant, would be able to cover for her on the weekend, and that her neighbor, Janet Ringling, would come to feed the cat, that she agreed. A road trip might be just the thing—graveyards or not.

And so Betty threw some things into a bag, they gassed up the Subaru, and drove to Jefferson's motel in Somerset to pick up his things. Now they were driving out along Glades Pike Road, also known as Route 31, through farmland and green forests, through the small town of Manns Choice, where Route 31 was called the Allegheny Road. Just outside of Bedford, 31 merged with Route 30: the Lincoln Highway. The road now more closely paralleled the Pennsylvania Turnpike. They might have saved 20 minutes by taking the turnpike from Somerset, but Jefferson instinctively opted for slower country roads whenever that was possible. In Pennsylvania, it was highly possible.

At Bedford, Jefferson kept to the right-hand fork where the old Lincoln Highway diverged from the new four-lane version of US 30. This led him to the outskirts of Bedford where he turned off on Telegraph Road and pulled up next to a small building shaped like a coffee pot.

"Of course you would want to stop here," said Betty. "But I don't think it's open for lunch anymore."

Jefferson never passed up an opportunity to gape at a "roadside attraction." This one was called the Koontz Coffee Pot and had been built in 1927 at the time when the Lincoln Highway was the only route through the Allegheny foothills. The Coffee Pot, a former lunch stand, had been restored and moved from Route 30 to its present location on the Bedford Fairgrounds only four years ago. It had been on the 2001 list of the Commonwealth of Pennsylvania's Most Endangered Historic Properties.

The Lincoln Highway, being the nation's first and oldest transcontinental highway, had fostered many examples of what came to be called "programmatic architecture." Buildings shaped like large tea pots, giant snails, huge rabbits, chickens, ducks, monumental shoes and such, popped up all over the country during the first part of the twentieth century. The Lincoln Highway through Pennsylvania had its share of oddities. One such marvel of programmatic architecture had been the S. S. Grand View Point Hotel, a large building perched precariously on the edge of the Allegheny Mountainside near Bedford, which resembled an ocean liner. It was also called "The Ship of the Alleghenies." It had boasted a vista of three states and seven counties, a decent restaurant and an open veranda. Its heyday had been in the decade of the 1930s but it had fallen into decline as a tourist attraction once the turnpike was opened in the 1940s. It sat empty for many years and burned to the ground in 2001.

Jefferson walked around the parameter of the Coffee Pot. Betty followed. "Why do you think we both imagined seeing that so-called ghost?" she asked. "I'm not prone to hallucinations."

"Nor am I. But I think it must have been the power of suggestion. You were telling me about the haunted hotel and I'd been thinking about dead soldiers and dead girls. You just picked up on my suggestion that there was a ghost image on the print of that man. Perhaps there was a defect in the printing paper which faded in time. There has to be a logical explanation."

"Where do we go from here?"

"We stay on old Route 30 until we see Route 26 to Huntingdon. We take that to a little town called Yellow Creek where there is a cemetery I want to walk and photograph. It's about an hour from here."

"How do you know about all these old cemeteries? They have to be pretty obscure."

"Google Earth. Ever hear of it? It's only been out for a few years for personal computers. They take all these satellite photographs of the earth and bind them together into a data base. You can 'fly' around the globe and zoom in as close as 15 meters. It's pretty cool. I'll show you later on my laptop."

They exited US 30 at Everette and swung through town to turn up Spring Street which became PA 26. Once clear of the town the road became more rural, spotted with farms and occasional small clusters of houses. Betty made a mental note to count the number of Brethren churches they passed. At Yellow Creek, one of those don't-blink-or-you'll-miss-it tiny hamlets, Jefferson made a sharp left turn up County Road 1024 and a right onto Jake's Corner Road. They pulled into the parking lot of the Bedford Forge Church.

"This looks awfully modern to be attracting you," said Betty. There was a nice Methodist Church and a good-sized cemetery right up against the road.

"You're right. I had thought it was abandoned," said Jefferson. "Let's look around anyway." He hoisted his tripod and camera bag and set off down to the opposite end of the cemetery. There they found a small cluster of very old graves: six in total.

"A family plot?"

"I think this part predates the more modern burial grounds. See the dates?" The newest burial was 1958, the oldest, 1909. The oldest birth date was 1840.

"Think we'll see any ghosts?" Betty asked. It was a joke—but she wasn't laughing.

10

The Valley of the Juniata

The road they traveled ran along the side of the Raystown Branch of the Juniata River, a tributary of the Susquehanna. Tree-covered ridges rose majestically on either side of this creating a deep water gap fed by small streams. At various localities, the ridges, some of them part of the Tussey Mountains, had different names: Huntingdon Mountain, Bald Eagle or Muncy Mountain, Williamsburg Mountain, Broad Top Mountain, Jack's Mountain, Black Top Mountain; and the lesser ridges were called Pine, Saddle Back, Blue, Sandy, Rocky, Chestnut, Allegrippus, Piney, Warrior's, and other names. So convoluted was the terrain that these individual ripples in the earth's surface were not seen as part of the same geography.

The fertile valleys attracted early German settlers; later the rich deposits of iron ore attracted the mining companies. The region's history dated to before the Revolutionary War; and there had been troubles with the indigenous peoples who had called the land home for a millennium. The young country grew and expanded, boomed and busted, and finally settled in to a tranquil, sparsely populated, sometimes fragile paradise where hard work was appreciated, expected, and sometime even rewarded. Some of those hard working people eventually drifted away.

They pulled off the road onto a grassy approach to the river and spread a blanket on the ground next to the Juniata's lapping shore. Betty had packed some sandwiches (ham salad on whole wheat), sweet gherkins, carrot sticks, seedless green grapes, and a can of Pringles. They had bought bottles of Snapple at a gas station; these were still cold. Large birds soared above them, riding subtle changes in the air currents. A cheeky squirrel approached, doubtlessly attracted by spilled crumbs; Jefferson held a Pringle out to it. The squirrel sniffed, seemed to turn up its nose (a bit of anthropomorphic nonsense, but it seemed that way to Jefferson), and it scurried away.

"Doesn't like sour cream and onions flavor, I guess."

Betty moved closer to Jefferson. Soon they both were lying on their backs, looking up at puffy clouds and describing to each other what sort of animals they resembled. "I could stay here forever," said Betty.

"We've got miles to go before we sleep, remember?"

"That's what you say, bud."

Betty rolled over on top of Jefferson. A long, intense kiss followed. Then another. Then they were side by side, arms entwined. Jefferson found himself slipping into a half-awake, half-asleep state where the billowing clouds took on their animal-like forms and gamboled and frisked to the sounds of the rushing river water. Sunlight filtered through rustling pine branches and danced across his drooping eyelids. Slumber came easily.

His shirt and the front of his pants were wet with blood. His hands felt sticky and he went to the sink to pump water. There, standing at the cast iron sink he thought to himself that his plan was working admirably. His wife would be the only heir to the farm with the rest of the family dead and buried. No longer would he need to struggle to make ends meet. No longer would he have to work running the farm for William Brown—a farm he deserved to own.

He carefully washed the blood from the blade of the axe. He hadn't needed to slash her throat with the axe blade; she was already dead from a fractured skull, the result of a heavy blow he had given her when her back was turned. This killing business was more difficult than he had thought it would be. He had hidden in the barn and waited for her to come to the front door of the house. His shot had struck her in the arm. She had screamed and staggered, but her wound was not fatal. He would have to finish her off before she could run away.

He couldn't read or write, but he was crafty. Luckily, she hadn't seen who had shot her. Once she reentered the house he ran swiftly from his hidey hole in the barn and came to where she was in the kitchen, wrapping her arm in a towel to stop the bleeding.

"Oh gawd, Miz Brown," he said to her. "What happened? Are you shot?"

Mrs. Brown was in a state of shock. She didn't recoil from him—good, then she didn't know it was he who had shot her. He led her into the bedroom, told her to rest while he went for the doctor. This was a lie: of course he would not go for a doctor. He would finish the job. His mother-in-law, Mrs. Brown, might bleed to death slowly—too slowly. He had other family members to take care of and he couldn't risk them knowing what he had done to Mrs. Brown. One by one he must isolate them. One by one he must eliminate them.

The first boy had been easy. He had simply told Jacob that the other boys were out back, playing Indian hunter. Jacob had run ahead of him on the path and he had felled him with a single shot. The bullet had entered the boy's brain and exited, taking pieces of his skull with it. He had covered the boy's body with leaves. Easy. He was not worried that the shot had echoed throughout the valley. Often shots were heard in this rural countryside. People hunted or shot vermin. The other family members would think little of it.

Yes, he was crafty. He had planned carefully. He had found a way to have the entire family in one place and at intervals so that the harvesting of their souls could be efficiently done. William Brown owned 160 acres on Jack's Mountain, operated a farm there, but worked at Matilda Furnace on the Juniata River opposite Mount Union. He would be returning to the farm late on Saturday. Thus he would be killed last. The oldest son, John, no longer lived with his parents, but worked on a neighboring farm. He had told John that a horse was for sale at his father's farm and that he might acquire it if he came early in the afternoon that Saturday. He would be the next to the last to depart this life.

That left the three boys, George, Jacob and David, the daughter, Elizabeth, and the wife, Roseanna. He had wanted to dispose of the three boys first. After killing Jacob he had hidden himself in the barn to wait for the other boys but they did not immediately appear. Elizabeth was helping her mother inside the house. He thought of a plan to separate the two women.

"Elizabeth," he said, speaking through the kitchen window, "I've found a nice patch of wild strawberries near the south field. Get you a bucket and come with me to gather them."

Elizabeth gladly obliged, bringing a tin bucket. She followed him to the field near where her brother's body lay covered with leaves and twigs. He picked up a large rock and struck her on her head, stunning her. Again he struck, and again. She fell to the ground, blood gushing from a deep gash on her forehead. He placed his foot against her throat and pushed, strangling her. Then he covered her body with leaves and small sticks.

Was he a cold-blooded killer? Did it bother him that he had just murdered a 17 year old girl, and brutally at that? Was it any different than butchering a hog for its meat or shooting coyotes that threatened the chickens? He felt no remorse, no shock of recognition that his deeds had been maleficent, horrifying, evil...

He waited again in the barn. The log construction left wide spaces through which he could peer; he stuffed straw in most of these to block view of himself from the outside, leaving just enough open area for his eyes, eyes that searched and waited for the two remaining boys to appear. Then George wandered across the yard, headed for the house. He called to the boy, telling him he had found a warren of rabbits up the hill. "Come quickly, we'll have a feast for supper," he said.

George would be found later, his skull crushed, both bones in his right arm broken, his jaw dislocated and his head and neck chewed by some animal. He had strangled the boy after beating him senseless. The youngest child, David, he had killed in a similar manner, beaten and strangled and left to the elements and the coyotes. He had first wounded him with bullet to the leg as he had run, then taken a stick to him. Four children were dead. He returned to the barn.

Now Roseanna Brown was bending over her bedside, woozy from the blood she had lost. He found an axe leaning against the side of the house. It would be a good idea, he thought, to save his bullets for the elder son, John, and for William Brown, who were yet to arrive. Gripping the axe and breathing heavily, he stole into the bedroom and swung! The axe opened a wound above her right eye and the force of the blow fractured her skull, killing her instantly. She was slumped on the bed. Taking no chances, he drew the blade of the axe across her juggler. The blade was dull and this took some force to execute.

After cleaning the axe and placing it ceremoniously back in its resting place against the side of the house, he fastened all the windows and shut the front door, removing the handle so that it could not be opened. He went to the cabin where he stayed, just a few yards down the drive. There he washed and changed clothes. Earlier that day he had taken his wife and children up the mountain to his mother's home for, he told them, a visit. He did not want them to witness what it was he had planned for the day. Next he returned to the barn to wait for John.

He had been squirreled away in his hiding place in the barn for several hours, content to chew tobacco and whittle on a piece of wood with his knife. John Brown arrived at the farm by horseback around 2 PM. Now it was time to act. He watched as John dismounted, tied his horse to the nearby fence and approached the front door of the house. The handle was missing. John stood, puzzled, not

58

understanding what was happening. He turned to search around the back of the house for his father and mother when a bullet struck him in the chest, passed through his body and lodged in the door jam. John tried to run toward the barn but fell dead before getting there.

He dragged John's body into the house and pushed it under the bed upon which Roseanna Brown lay in a pool of congealing blood. He found ten dollars in John's pocket…money John had intended to use to buy the horse from his father…the horse that didn't exist. He searched throughout the house and found the chest where William Brown kept his money. He took what he found there. It would tide him over until the will was read and his wife inherited the farm. He returned to the barn to await the final member of the doomed family: William Brown.

Brown had walked ten miles from his job at Matilda Furnace to get to his home. He was carrying an iron skillet and a sledge hammer, which were tied together and slung over his shoulder. It was a hot day and the walk had taken him over ten hours. When he reached his house he was, of course, unaware that all of his immediate family lay dead and that a vicious killer was waiting for him in the barn. He got to the door which he had expected to find open but it was closed tight and the handle was missing. This and the ominous silence sent a chill up his spine. Suddenly, a shot rang out.

He had been waiting and now the final victim was in his sights. He aimed carefully this time, not wanting to wound but to kill. He squeezed the trigger slowly, the way his own father had taught him so many years ago on his first hunting trip. This time he was hunting for human game, game that was capable of fighting back. He couldn't take the chance that Brown might run away or retaliate against him. His aim was good, but just at that moment, Brown moved and the bullet, instead finding flesh, struck against the iron skillet and ricocheted into the door.

"You damned rascal! What are you doing there?" Brown cried.

He ran. Had Brown recognized him? He was stumbling, making for the wooded area down the road, his breath coming in gasps. He could hear footsteps behind him. He crashed through brambles into the woods, branches scraping his skin. He fell once, twisted an ankle, but a surge of fear flowed through him, spurring him on. Now he was panting, sweat rolling down his face. The trees were becoming more dense…closing in on him.

Jefferson woke in a sweat, his breath coming hard and fast. What a horrible dream, he thought. To be the protagonist of a mass murder! He sat up, caught his breath, saw that Betty was still sleeping.

They had slept for most of the afternoon and now he was way behind schedule. He still couldn't quite shake the emotions that the dream had conjured. He would wait until his head cleared, then wake her. They had miles to go before they could sleep.

11

Standing Stones Gather Much Moss

The Standing Stone stood in the center of a small park-like island in the middle of Penn Street in Huntingdon, Pennsylvania, the town where Jefferson and Betty had terminated their day's journey. Jefferson had parked the Subaru across from it and they walked over to take a look. It appeared to be a war memorial from the cluster of American flags and associated square rocks emblazoned with the insignias of American Veterans' groups that surrounded it. But a little research on the internet (which Jefferson would do later that night) would reveal the stone monument's long and storied history.

This was at least the third version of the stone. The city of Huntingdon was laid out in 1776 by Rev. Dr. William Smith on the site of an earlier Native American settlement; the exact spot was said to have been a sacred council ground for the Oneida, Tuscarora, Seneca and Susquehannock peoples. At this place, where the Stone Creek emptied into the Juniata River, the Native Americans had erected their stone. It had been a tall (perhaps as tall as fourteen feet), slim (perhaps tapering from sixteen inches at the base to eight inches at the top), square monolith intended by the original inhabitants to mark their territory. Accounts by early settlers noted that its surface was covered with "hieroglyphics" which seemed to be used to record the Native Americans' history. When the Native Americans were supplanted by the European settlers, they took the stone with them.

According to J. Simpson Africa's *History of Huntingdon and Blair Counties*, 1883 (Jefferson had read), "…another stone was erected by the whites on the site of the original one, and was accidentally broken by a misthrow in the play of 'long-bullets.' Upon it, beside many cabalistic characters, were cut the names of John Lukens (with the date 1768), Charles Lukens, Thomas Smith, and others." A fragment of this second Standing Stone was displayed in the lobby of the present Huntingdon County courthouse. The inscriptions "J. Lukens" and "1768" were clearly visible on it.

A third stone was erected during Huntingdon Borough's Centennial celebration in September 1896 in order to honor, as J. Simpson Africa said in his address at that celebration, "recollections of the toils, dangers and privations suffered by our fathers in their labors to build homes here, on the bank of the peerless Juniata." Perhaps it was not so much to honor the memory of the original inhabitants, the "Standing Stone Peoples," however.

Jefferson had taken note of two poems that accompanied the document of Africa's centennial address. The first, called "The Blue Juniata," by Mrs. Marion Dix Sullivan (1802-1860) began with the verse:

> *Wild roved an Indian girl,*
> *Bright Alfarata,*
> *Where sweep the waters*
> *Of the Blue Juniata;*
> *Swift as an antelope,*
> *Through the forest going.*
> *Loose were her jetty locks*
> *In wavy tresses flowing.*

And the second, "A Response to The Blue Juniata," by Rev. Cyrus Cort, D. D. (b 1865) which began:

> *The Indian girl has ceased to rove*
> *Along the winding river;*
> *The warrior Brave that won her love.*
> *Is gone, with bow and quiver.*

> *The valley rears another race,*
> *Where flows the Juniata;*
> *Where maidens rove, with paler face*
> *Than that of Alfarata.*

They had found food and lodging in Huntingdon and had settled down in their motel room, Betty reading a novel and Jefferson researching the area on his laptop. He had discovered the documents outlining the history of the Standing Stone and of the area. And he was locating old cemeteries—many old cemeteries—more than enough to satisfy his wanderlust and enrich his database. There was a mini bar; Betty unscrewed the top of a miniature bottle of Rosé.

"Want some?" she asked.

"No…thanks anyway. Look, I think we'll head down to Shirleysburg tomorrow. There's a promising looking cemetery in the German Valley there. An old Brethren burial ground near where one of the first churches was built. I guess the old church is gone now."

"That dream you told me about? It gave me the creeps."

"It gave *you* the creeps! It was amazingly vivid. And I was surprised I remembered it in such detail. Usually dreams are pretty foggy after you wake up. After I wake up, anyway."

"No, that's true. Are you sure you didn't read a story somewhere and it was just popping into your memory banks?"

"That could be. You know what…I'm going to do a search on that name…Brown. Let's see what I can find."

"That's an awfully common name."

"Yes, I guess you're right."

But he felt a compulsion to pursue the idea that there might be some truth to the dream. Perhaps he *had* read about the murders during his research. He didn't remember having done so. He brought up Google and typed "Brown Cemetery" into the search box. Sometimes there were family cemeteries when a large number of members of the same family lived—and died—together in rural locales. He pressed the "enter" key.

Sometimes, when using the search engine, you had to look through dozens of pages of links before you found a relevant one. He narrowed the search by adding "Pennsylvania" and "old." He found it.

In 1755, due to the advent of the French and Indian Wars, a series of stockades appeared in the forested country west of the Susquehanna. These became known as Fort Shirley, after the general who oversaw them. The Township of Shirley and the Borough of Shirleysburg came soon after. As the small community grew it attracted many people of German and Scots-Irish descent, often recent immigrants. There arose saw mills and grist mills and a terracotta works, a distillery, a tannery and the usual stores providing necessities and niceties to the settlers. There came physicians, blacksmiths, wheelwrights, tailors, tavern keepers, and many who wished to farm the fertile valley. One of the earliest churches to be built was the Shirleysburg Baptist Church, often referred to as the "Old Stone Church" because of its construction from local limestone.

The main street of the town was now Route 522 (there called Croghan Pike). There were only two other north-south streets: East Street and West Street, so houses and shops were laid out along these three avenues; Shirleysburg proper was only about five or six blocks long. Jefferson turned off of Croghan Pike onto a road designated as Trail 509; indeed, it had been an old trail. This stretched northeast along Fort Run and then angled back southeasterly into the German Valley. At the junction with Loves Valley Road, Jefferson came upon the German Valley Cemetery, once associated with the Old Stone Church, then abandoned, and now collecting new generations to await Gabriel's trumpet.

They unpacked the camera gear and wandered through the cemetery grounds, searching for the oldest sections. Here Jefferson found the names of some of the original settlers caved on the headstones: Cornelius, Lutz, Eby, Smelker, Myers—even a woman named Brown—no relationship to the Browns of his dream, however. Betty noticed that Jefferson seemed agitated during this photo shoot. It was an extensive cemetery but he recorded only this older section, then hurried back to the car. "Miles to go," he said.

From Route 522, just south of Shirleysburg, Jefferson turned onto a side road called Runk Road. This crossed the Aughwick Creek and brought them to Aughwick Creek Road, a picturesque byway that ran along the creek, following its every twist and turn. Aughwick Creek Road changed its name to McClure Road and swung southward but Jefferson turned off onto another country road called Colgate Road. All this navigation caused Betty to exclaim, "How in the world do you know where you're going?"

"Google Earth, remember? I found a deserted family cemetery I want to visit and memorized the directions from looking at the map."

They had left the heavily wooded area along Aughwick Creek and now the forest shared the terrain with small farms where trees had been cleared and fields had been plowed. Colgate Road ended in a "T" intersection with Route 747. Jefferson turned south and watched the odometer. Yes! At just about one quarter of a mile he saw a gravel road turning off into the woods. They had entered the northeastern edge of State Game Land 99. The turn-off ended abruptly at a gate, which was closed. Now they would have to hike some distance through the woods.

"Ugh! Mosquitoes!" exclaimed Betty.

They rarely bother me," said Jefferson. Vitamin D or something like that." He handed Betty the tripod to carry.

"Slave driver! Torturer by insect bites! You're obsessed…this is the forest primeval…with the emphasis on 'evil.' "

Not far from where the access road had entered the park they came upon a parking lot. Jefferson had expected a trailhead, but nothing presented itself. "Now we search," he said.

"We should be wearing orange vests," said Betty. "This is a *game* park. People shoot at anything that moves."

"Well, just don't act like a deer and you'll be OK."

Jefferson used the center of the parking area as a reference point and began walking into the woods in one direction at a time, boxing the compass. He was certain the cemetery wasn't far from the parking area. Betty trudged after him for the first several probes into the brush, but then sat down in the middle of the open area where she could practice not acting like a deer. When Jefferson reached SSW in his boxing, he found a rudimentary path through the woods—not exactly a trail, but it had been used by something other than wildlife, and recently.

"Come on," he said. "I think I've found it."

Betty stood up, hefted the tripod and followed, hoping that either Jefferson had found the cemetery, or that it didn't exist and that this fact would soon become apparent. It wasn't really any fun any more. Not for her.

It wasn't far from the road, just as Jefferson had figured. There it was, an unkempt low hill clear of trees but covered with a thick blanket of weeds. He could make out six graves. At one end of the burial ground a large slab of limestone was standing—a standing stone to mark the sad occasion of the internment of a family. He read the inscription on the stone:

Byron Grush

Here lies The Brown family
slain by Robert McConahy on May 1840
Rosannah aged 51 years
   John . . 19 years
   Betsy . . 18 years
   George . . 16 years
   Jacob . . 14 years
   David . . 11 years

12

Schizotypy is Painless

A young girl pedaled her bicycle down the sidewalk in front of Betty Snyder's house. The training wheels were not adjusted properly and the bike wobbled a little. Jefferson and Betty watched from the porch glider; it was almost a Norman Rockwell moment—except it wasn't. Jefferson had brought Betty home after a minor disharmony at the pizza place in Three Springs where they had stopped for lunch after photographing the Brown Family Cemetery.

"You're really freaking me out," Betty had told him. "I think it's time for me to go home and you to go on your own way. Alone."

"I'm sure I must have read about the murders when I was researching on the internet, Betty. That's the only plausible explanation." Jefferson was certain there *was* an explanation—only he was equally certain he hadn't read about the murders. He had Googled every combination of the words "murders," "Brown family," "Huntingdon," and so forth, and gotten exactly zero hits. How could he have read about it?

Now they had returned to Windber and Betty had mellowed about Jefferson leaving. He could stay, but there was no way she would accompany him on any more sorties after burial sites. She needed to return to her duties at the museum. The prints from the glass negatives were due back from the framer and she wanted to announce their showing to the museum's supporters.

"Do you watch much television, Jeff?" she asked, pushing the glider slowly with her sandaled foot.

"I watch very little. Just, ah, 'Star Trek' and the 'Simpsons'…oh, and the 'PBS News Hour.' Can't stand network or cable news. Too jaded."

"Have you ever watched a show called 'Medium?' With Patricia Arquette?"

"Um…a couple times. That and the 'X Files.' But I like my science fiction with bug-eyed aliens."

"Did you know that there is a real Allison DuBois that Arquette's character is based on? That she claims to be a medium and a clairvoyant and works with the police to solve crimes, just like in the TV show?"

"What's your point? You think I should go talk to this medium person?"

"No…no, I'm not saying that. I'm just thinking that there are people who study this stuff. Parapsychologists."

"Parapsychology is a pseudoscience. No one in the scientific world takes it seriously. Most mediums are found to be frauds and the research into the phenomenon is shown to be flawed. I don't buy it."

"I'm not selling it. But, there is one of the museum members who knows a lot about this stuff. Rodney Blount. I could invite him for dinner or drinks or something."

"Betty, really…I don't think so. It's just…hallucinations or something. Too much scrapple."

"Ugh! How can you eat that crap? Yes, that's probably it. You're hallucinating from too much scrapple. Somebody put magic mushrooms in it. Or maybe we're both crazy. I saw the ghost image in the photograph too, remember? I saw the evidence of the murders written on that monument…and how could you have remembered that story so accurately?"

"We don't know what the real story was. I got the names right, though, didn't I? Pretty psychic of me, I'd say."

"Don't you have a level?" Jefferson asked. He had been busy measuring and marking the wall with pencil where nails would be pounded for hanging the framed photographs.

"Can't you just eye-ball it?" Betty responded. "This isn't the Louvre."

"You think I'm obsessive-compulsive, don't you?"

"Hmmm."

This repartee was interrupted by the dinging of the small bell that hung over the museum's front door to announce visitors. Betty called out, "We're not open just yet." But the visitor entered the room where Jefferson and Betty were hanging pictures anyway.

"Rod!" Betty cried and embraced the man with a hug that Jefferson perceived as particularly intense and obviously personal. Long lost brother? Prodigal lover?

"Jefferson, this is Rodney Blount, an old friend. I invited him to look at the photos today because he is going out of town during the opening."

Middle to late forties (Jefferson guessed) with prematurely graying hair cut long (but at least there wasn't the "old man pony tail" sported by some of that age group), casually but neatly dressed, and a man who probably worked out or at least ran several miles every day—everything a reluctantly jealous person could want in a new acquaintance! Jefferson took the hand that was offered and shook it, squeezing a bit harder than necessary. His strong grip was returned in kind. "Just here to see the pictures?" he said, more as a statement to taunt than as an inquiry to learn.

"Betty told me about you," Blount answered. "I'm very interested in…unusual events, and I hoped to get your insight into your experiences. Please, let me take the two of you to dinner tonight. We can relax and talk."

"Oh, please, Jeff? I have a lot to catch up with Rod and I think you'll like each other."

"Okay, but it has to be Dutch treat," Jefferson answered. He was hooked; he couldn't say no to Betty, not after she had obviously gone to some trouble to arrange this (fortuitous?) meeting. Arranged without his permission…but she meant well. Didn't she?

They met at Patti's on 15th Street. Betty had recommended it as an old established family style place that served good, inexpensive Italian fare and was reasonably quiet (a major criteria for Jefferson who hated noisy restaurants). Drinks were ordered: a frosted mug of Yuengling for Jefferson, a bottle of Rolling Rock for Rodney Blount, and a glass of Lambrusco for Betty. An appetizer of fried zucchini followed. While they waited for their soup, salad and entrees (cups of wedding soup and antipasto for all, and fettuccine with red clam sauce for Betty, vegetable lasagna for Rodney, and a filet mignon wrapped in bacon for Jefferson), Rodney explained something of his background for Jefferson's benefit:

"2001 saw me at the University of Arizona working on a masters in psychology. While I was there I had occasion to work in what we called 'the lab,' the Human Energy Systems Laboratory. I took some seminars with Doctor Gary Schwartz who headed up the VERITUS Research Program for Survival and Medium Research. He believes in the possibilities for communication at various spiritual levels in addition to those we commonly experience through our physical senses.

"He is an interesting guy. He claimed his interest in psychic phenomenon started when he was driving with his wife on the FDR freeway in Manhattan. He had pulled over to the side of the road and a voice told him to put his seat belt on. He and his wife did so and with in a few minutes, their car was back-ended by a speeding car. It was so vivid an experience he decided to research the paranormal. He left Harvard (where his new research wasn't appreciated) and talked his way into the Department of Psychology at U of Arizona. I worked under him at the time he conducted psychic testing with Allison DuBois."

"I knew it," blurted Jefferson. "More hocus pocus. I don't believe I saw any ghosts or dreamed an experience from the past, Mr. Blount. I am a skeptic and you'll not convince me otherwise."

"It's Rodney…please. And bear with me. I am as skeptical as you are…probably more so. Let me finish."

The antipasto had come and Betty was giving Jefferson one of *those* looks. Jefferson took a large swallow of his beer and settled back in his chair. "Okay," he said. "Sorry. It is a bit unnerving to think you've seen a ghost, even when you don't believe in them."

"Apparitional experience. We don't like to use the term, 'ghost' if we can avoid it. And you should realize that it is the most intelligent of people who are the most suggestive to strangeness. Have you ever head the term, 'schizotypy?' Sometimes referred to as psychosis-proneness."

"You think I'm schizophrenic? I'm batty?"

"No…no. There is a spectrum…a dimensional framework, if you will, of personality, in which we can observe the occurrence of hallucinations in normal, non-psychotic personalities. That is, it is possible to have 'real' (here Rodney made quote signs with his fingers in the air) experiences that have the character of sense perception, but without actual sensory stimulation. What we see does not have any direct contact with the external world, but appears to do so. And at the healthy end of the spectrum."

"You're still saying I'm a wacko."

"Well, spiritualists would say that what you saw was the result of external spirit agencies…proof of the after life. The energy that is the life force remains after leaving the body and attempts to make its way through the various levels of reality on its way to heaven. All paranormal activity is the result of spirits trying to communicate with the living."

"And what do you think?"

"About Spiritualism? I agree with Michael Shermer. You've heard of him of course? He wrote *Why People Believe Weird Things* and other wonderful treatises on skepticism. He says there are two kinds of errors in thinking: believing in a falsehood and rejecting a truth. Spiritualists fall into the first category. Things like clairvoyance, psi, ESP, and psychokinesis violate the second law of thermodynamics and several other well established scientific principles. Believers in these things fall into the second category. And apparitional phenomena? That presupposes the existence of ghosts, for which there is absolutely no proof whatsoever. So."

"And this Gary Schwartz? What was his conclusion about Allison DuBois?"

"Oh, he said she was 73 percent accurate, enough to warrant his assertion that there was *something* going on that wasn't fraudulent. He believed she could contact deceased persons."

"You think I'm channeling dead people when I have these experiences?"

"If we assume the schizotypy view that there is a spectrum of personality where a normal person is prone to perceptual anomalies which are not the result of latent psychosis and, obviously, not the result of spirit interference, then it would be beneficial to examine these phenomena more closely. I would very much like to work with you on a few…experiments. I think you would find it interesting, and I assure you, I am no quack or fraud or seeker of notoriety."

The entrees arrived just in time to forestall Jefferson's answer. Betty was giving him that look again. Did he want to be a guinea pig for some pseudo-scientific, new-age-has-been, (way too handsome to be around Betty very long), P. T. Barnum-esque, psycho-tripping user who might analyze him, hypnotize him, traumatize him, demoralize him? He did not. But Betty…and the look…

"Um, what did you have in mind?" he answered.

13

The Barnum Effect

On a shelf behind the desk in Blount's Johnstown office sat an array of carved wooden elephants; six in number, they varied in size from about ten inches in length to about three, and were arranged in a line in order of size. They were made of a dark-stained mahogany and all had tusks of some white material that Jefferson imagined was real ivory. Illegal to sell anything made of ivory unless it is very, very old, thought Jefferson. This made him think about Rodney Blount as someone who placed himself above, or at least outside of the socially conscious, politically correct personality typical of highly educated people (liberals)—particularly those devoted to the study of human behavior—and this thought was both disturbing and intriguing.

"I have a small private practice where I counsel people in dysfunctional relationships. I'm not a psychiatrist, you understand, just a glorified social worker that charges enough money to give people the idea that I'm an authority," explained Blount. "It attracts people who have expectations of resolution, and therefore are able to work through their problems, believing my guidance has made a difference. It's easy money and I do it to support my research, for which I could never get any support academically or from industry. You probably think me unethical, but the results usually satisfy my clients and leave me plenty of free time for the important stuff."

"Wow," said Jefferson. "The spice of life."

"What's that? Oh…cynicism. Yes, certainly it is a cynical approach to a so-called professional career. Have you ever heard of 'the Barnum effect?' No? It is the predisposition of people to accept arbitrary and minimal information which appeals to their needs, wants and personal beliefs. It is the same principle that works for palm readers and phony spirit mediums. You come close to guessing something about them and they fill in the rest because the *want* to believe you are clairvoyant or at least sensitive to their undiscovered selves."

Jefferson leaned back in the old-fashioned wooden chair he was seated in and was delighted to find it was spring-loaded and would recline to a comfortable position. It did make a sort of squeaking noise, as if to complain, but this added to the homeliness of Jefferson's repose.

"You are trying to tell me, I gather, not to trust you, take anything you say to heart, or follow your advice, unless I can be absolutely positive that my revelations come from my own introspection and not from your suggestions however coincidental they may be," said Jefferson.

"You, sir, are in the wrong profession. You should have studied psychology."

"I read a lot of Alan Watts."

"How about C. G. Jung? His theories of synchronicity? He talks about an 'acausal connecting principle' which basically means things can be connected by *meaning* where there is no causal relationship, especially when any causal connection is inconceivable. He called it synchronicity."

"So do we find meaning in disparate synchronic events, or are the events synchronic because they have a similar meaning?"

"Yes."

"Well," said Jefferson, summoning his inner cynical angels, "Watts said that reality was really only a Rorschach ink-blot."

"And he said trying to understand yourself was like trying to bite your own teeth. But we are here to talk about you. Actually, not about you so much as about your abilities, whatever they may be or not be. Do you know about the Zenner card deck? The one that was used a lot in the 70's to try to prove ESP existed?"

"The ones with the square, the circle…"

"The cross, the star, and the waves. You can call the shapes anything you like. They were chosen to be simple, graphically different from each other, and easy to describe. They came in a deck with five of each card and were shuffled. The subject would try to guess which of the five shapes the interviewer was looking at behind a wooden shield. Obviously, by random chance, the subject would be right 20 percent of the time, with a one in five chance of guessing correctly. The idea was to find individuals who could get beyond that percentage.

"Zenner and a man named Joseph Rhine did a lot of testing with the cards in the 30s but their findings were disputed. Apparently fault was found where clues could be given by facial gestures, or the designs determined through their reflections in the interviewer's glasses…that sort of thing. Petty complaints, but the system was more or less dropped except by New Age practitioners and their ilk. The use of cards was compared to a stage magician's deck and the findings to tricks of legerdemain.'"

"But?"

"The theory itself isn't faulty. If you can show a success well above the statistical average of 20 percent, you may have an indication of…something. Synchronicity perhaps. And whatever the subject's ability may be with the cards, it might be applicable to other sensory anomalies."

"Like seeing ghosts or reliving past lives."

"Apparitional experiences, remote viewing, channeling…yes. All of the above."

"But the flaws…"

"This is the age of computers, is it not? I have a program which randomly generates the Zenner designs and lets you predict which it has come up with before seeing it. You alone run the program. There is no chance for clues from an interviewer or sloppy shuffling or anything else. I video tape you using the program and we tabulate the results. We repeat it several times and calculate an average of accuracy for you…an ESP index, if you will. So are you game?"

"Why sure. Sounds like fun. Bring it on," Jefferson said aloud. To himself he thought, "This will be boring. Hope I don't fall asleep."

Actually, he was getting drowsy. They had been at it now for six straight hours, Jefferson hunched over the computer screen and Blount working his camera remotely from an adjoining room. The first session had been disappointing for Jefferson. He had imagined he would be found to possess extraordinary psychic abilities. But he had scored only 22.2 percent—hardy significant. A blank card would appear on the screen along with five images of the Zenner cards. He would decide which of the designs were on the blank card and click his mouse over the corresponding Zenner image. This was repeated 25 times to represent the scope of the Zenner deck, each new card being randomly generated by the program. The score was totaled and the percentage of correct guesses displayed on the monitor. Then it began again.

He was on session number 20. Several dips and some slight gains in his accuracy had been made in each progressive session up to number 15, then his percentages had dropped below the normal range. Fatigue was setting in. He let loose of his concentration on the cards and entered into a sort of day-dreaming state in which he was still able to function in the test, but on a more intuitive and automatic level. At the end of session 20 his average popped up on the screen: 40 percent.

He snapped back to attention, pleased with his success and concentrated once again upon picking the cards. Circle, wavy lines, circle, cross, square, star, wavy lines.... But at the finish of session 21 he was appalled by his result: zero. He hadn't made one correct guess out of 25 attempts! Now Blount entered the room.

"Jefferson," he said, "what did you do differently in the last two sessions? I could see a change in your body language in session 20...you seemed more relaxed. Then..."

"I think it has to do with letting my mind drift. Like day-dreaming or the automatic writing of the surrealists. Let me try again."

And now Jefferson did empty his mind and give himself over to a semi-conscious state. And his results were extraordinary—40, 50, 80 percent! A steady increase in accuracy that defied random chance. He was so tired that he nearly fell asleep and so Blount called the sessions to an end.

"I think I could have gotten it up to 100 percent," Jefferson told Blount.

"If we take *all* the sessions and average them together, we still only get 23.6 percent. Just barely above average and not a significant anomaly to write home about. I think, however, that you have discovered something about your perceptivity in different states of consciousness. I'd like to try something tomorrow. You go home and get some rest and come back early tomorrow. I want to try hypnotism."

Jefferson had picked the lead elephant as an object on which to focus while Blount talked him into a hypnotic state. He had expected to be staring at a swinging pocket watch but, well, it was only in the movies where the evil scientist, played by Bela Lugosi, would coax our hero into a zombie-like trance—ah, those deep-set, soul-haunting eyes—that reassuring baritone ("you are falling azleeeb…")—that enveloping darkness like a cloak thrown over you as you sink—

"Deeper…deeper…now you are *so* relaxed…you can let go of your conscious mind…let any visions come to you…open yourself…"

The elephant was doing a little dance. The others were joining in. This is really silly, Jefferson thought to himself. I can't be hypnotized. My will is too strong. Blount will see that he is mistaken. Wait. Was that water he heard? The sound of surging, plummeting, cascading water! Many tons of liquid fury were rushing into the room, filling it with foaming, swirling whirlpools of rank, smelling, bath-like flecked water with filthy flotsam that assailed the senses—what was *that* that floated by, taunting him with its human-like visage? The peeled skin revealing ruptured muscle, shattered bone—the glaring, lidless eyes that pierced into your soul, beckoning, pleading, accusing.

He was running now. The deluge was swallowing buildings, bridges. A whole train—locomotive, cars, caboose—was rolling, sinking, dashed against pylons. Houses swirled like leaves in a pool of spring rain. Behind him, a building collapsed. He saw people jumping from windows, clinging to splintered furniture that spun and careened in the flood, men with arms and legs flailing, floating face down, a mother grasping her baby, no longer able to struggle, a horrible torrent to wash away humanity and all its works, an inundation paramount to that first biblical flood, but with no ark to arrive in time to save the righteous.

The rising water reached him, clutched at his ankles. It pushed at him, pulled at him, buffeted him like a wash rag in a washtub. He scrambled, hugged a tree—the tree was wrenched, roots and all, from the soggy turf, was thrown into the cataract and he with it. Over and under they rolled. He swallowed, retched, gagged. His tree raft was flung up onto high ground—a miracle. He lay in a heap, trying to force the screams of the town from his ears.

"Where are you? What do you see?"

"Johnstown. It is May, 1889. The damn has broken and the river is carrying a wall of debris down the valley. The town is being destroyed by the huge wave. The people…oh, it's horrible. People are standing on rooftops. Then the buildings collapse into the tide. There's a small child being carried away by the rush of the water. I don't want to be here, to see this. Get me back!"

14

The Exhibition

Betty had hung a banner from the second floor balcony at the museum. It said: "Exhibition of 19th Century Period Photographs." She had placed an advertisement in the local paper announcing an opening for the show, free to the public (Sunday, 2 to 5 PM). The framed photos she and Jefferson had hung looked very impressive in the setting of the museum. And now the day had come. She had cleared an antique table of its artifacts and set a plate of home-made cookies and a thermos of hot coffee on it. She hoped to acquire some new members for the museum, to generate interest within the Windber community, and to collect some donations.

Sally Pleasant, Betty's co-worker at the museum, had dressed in a 19th century costume: floor-length skirt belled out by crinoline, a ribbon tying up her hair. Betty wore a less flamboyant outfit, still reminiscent of yesteryear, but considerably more practical; Sally took up a lot of space in the small front room of the museum. Jefferson had found an antique view camera in the museum's collection, complete with wooden tripod and black viewing cloth. He had set this up in a corner, doffed a moldy smelling bowler hat, also from the collection, and pretended to photograph people as they arrived at the show.

The Windber Garden Club had rallied its members, and four of the ladies came early, managed to gobble up about half of the cookies, oo-ed and ah-ed at the photos, and disappeared as suddenly as they had appeared. The balance of the club filtered in one by one throughout the afternoon. Betty spoke to each, giving an account of the discovery of the glass plates and the process by which she and Jefferson had produced the prints.

Most of the museum's membership came. There were many congratulatory utterances but few close inspections of the black and white images that graced the walls. In fact, no one seemed to exhibit more than a casual interest in the photos. Odd, thought Jefferson. As photographs they ranged from stunning to extraordinary. As artifacts of the past they were windows into a world lost even to memory—for no one alive had been in those places at those times—at least, Jefferson mused, not physically.

Jefferson studied the photo of the Civil War soldier once more. The eager face that couldn't begin to imagine the horrors it would behold. The confident grip on the musket—one could imagine the swagger in the step, the tipping of the hat upon meeting a representative of the fair sex, the rigid stance at the muster before boarding the train that would take him and his fellows off to parade before the President, the pathos of acceptance of duty and fate so characteristic of the young, of the Universal Soldier. The Universal Soldier without whom there could be no war. No war, no battlefields, no mass graves.

He moved to the next photograph, a seated portrait of a woman. Sally Pleasant came up to him as he studied the expression on the woman's face: one of passivity, boredom even—of course the exposures were long and the poses necessarily stiff. Sally had met Jefferson before. She commented on the picture ("An uptight old bitty"). Then she said:

"I hear you've met Betty's friend, Rodney. I bet that was uncomfortable."

"What do you mean?" Jefferson asked, perplexed, and not anxious to hear the discouraging answer he knew was coming.

"Only that I used to think maybe they were...an item. But then you came along and guess you became the flavor of the day."

"The flavor of...aren't you being a little critical of Betty? She isn't like that...flirtatious or whatever you're implying. Maybe you're the one who is jealous?"

"Just sayin'. You just see what you want to see," she said, and walked away, leaving Jefferson smoldering.

I never liked that girl, Jefferson thought to himself. Flavor of the day? He moved to the next picture. This one showed two children, girls who could have been twins, standing. One of the girls looked peculiar. On closer examination, Jefferson determined that the girl in question was deceased; it was a often the practice to photograph a deceased person in a "living pose" and in this case, the girl's sister stood next to her to create an image of remembrance for the family. Bizarre. Macabre. But during that time, a photograph was so unique (and expensive) that it became the perfect memorial to express one's grief for the departed. Gone but not forgotten, immortalized in blackened silver on glossy paper.

The photos had been framed well, properly matted with archival paper mattes, but Betty had saved some money by opting for regular instead of non-glare glass. Thus the room and the movements of people in it were reflected in the frame glass. This necessitated positioning oneself to minimize reflective interference when viewing the photographs.

And thus it was that Jefferson now moved to the next photo, which happened to be the man in the chair, the same photo in which, briefly, they had seen a ghostly shape. Jefferson was annoyed that this photograph in particular seemed to reflect the room behind him no matter at what angle he viewed it. In a way, he thought, it was appropriate that this one photo should contain these "ghostly" images—it had been the object that had instigated the series of strange visions he had had, and it was comforting…even humorous…to know that the source of the "ghosts," at least this time, was the movement of the very real, very alive visitors to the museum this afternoon.

In fact, he began to "play" with angles that would bring the reflection of this person or that person into the position on the photograph where he and Betty had seen their ghost. He had Sally and her bulging skirt sitting on the man's lap until she moved out of range. That was funny. Now a tall man in a white shirt moved right into the empty area above the man's prop table, just at the position the original ghost had occupied. And now Jefferson no longer was amused by the game, for this man wore something else white— something that stood out against his forehead. Jefferson turned around.

Behind him stood the man who had been reflected in the photo. His head was bandaged. Jefferson blinked. The man stepped forward toward him. He spoke casually, matter-of-factly, as if they were old friends:

"You are the photographer that helped Betty with the photographs," the man said. "How do you do. My name is Alan Tinsley. I'm one of the charter members here. We appreciate all the help you given our Betty."

"I, uh…I'm sorry, I didn't mean to stare."

"Oh, the bandage? Had a nasty fall this morning. Hit the old noggin and bled all over the place. Doc fixed me up, pumped me full of Vicodin and stitched me up real good…stapled me up, I should say. These days they…"

"Excuse me. I need to talk to Betty right now. Nice meeting you."

Jefferson moved away from the man, oblivious to having essentially snubbed him. But he felt nauseous. Was this just another example of synchronicity? He had the ominous feeling that the man was familiar—too familiar. It wasn't just the similarity of a man in a white shirt with a bandage on his head to the ghostly image of a robed man with a turban. There was something more. It was as if this man had walked out of a dream, a dream he *was going to have*.

He found Betty carrying a fresh tray of cookies from the museum's kitchen. "Can we go somewhere and talk?" he asked. "Just for a few minutes."

"You look kind of pale. Let's go out on the second flood balcony and get some air. Nobody is supposed to be out there. And Jefferson? Get rid of that stupid hat."

"Wait. Look. You see that man over there? Do you know him?"

"Yes, of course. That's Alan Tinsley. He's one of our…"

"Charter members. Yes, I know. I think I might have been short with him. Cut him off in mid sentence and walked away from him."

"We'll apologize to him later. Right now, follow me."

The balcony was old and looked rickety, but Betty assured Jefferson it was in good shape. There was a nice view of the street and of the old municipal building, that is, if you liked old municipal buildings.

"I kind of freaked when I saw that Tinsley fellow's refection in the picture glass. I was looking at the photo of our old friend, the Professor. Tinsley appeared right where the ghost had been…and he had that bandage on his head."

"Jeff, you're getting to be more and more paranoid. You've got to just relax."

"It's when I relax that the trouble starts. The visions come. Memories I couldn't possibly have. People I couldn't possibly have known about. Paranoid? Maybe. And speaking of paranoid…"

He stepped back from her. There was a lull while they looked into each other's eyes, searching for meaning, searching for reassurance, searching for depth of feeling and mutual trust. Jefferson spoke first:

"I was talking to Sally. She hinted that you and Blount were…"

"An item? Why that little…. No, Jefferson. Rodney helped me right after Brian died in Afghanistan. Talked me through a really bad depression. I saw him professionally."

"And socially?"

"A few times, yes. He is a sweet man. Very supportive. Very trustworthy. He would never…"

"You trusted him enough to recommend him to me. He warned me about seeing him as a sort of guru or miracle worker. Did he warn you about that? About the Barnum effect?"

"The what? No, I…I don't know, Jefferson. Please believe me, there is nothing between us. Like I said before, you are getting to be paranoid in your old age." She chuckled here, attempting to interject some levity into the confrontation. It only slightly worked, Jefferson cracking a smile, but turning to stare out over the balcony to watch squirrels chasing each other up the trucks of trees across the street.

"You've come to mean a lot to me," he finally said, still looking away from Betty. "I guess I'm just jealous." Now he turned around…but she was gone.

That night he checked into motel. Betty hadn't come home from the museum yet so he packed up his things and left. No note, no phone call. He needed to be alone to think. He imagined she felt the same way. He picked up a container of Kun Pau chicken from a local Chinese carryout. Washed it down with a warm bottle of Yuenling Lager. There was nothing better, he thought to himself, for when you're feeling sorry for yourself, than bad Chinese and warm beer.

His sleep was restless. Old reruns of M*A*S*H on the cable didn't help him to sleep. Eventually he did fall into a deep, dreamless sleep. Around 3 in the morning, however, sounds of partying in the room next door woke him. He tossed, he turned, he got up and opened another Yuenling, downed it swiftly, crawled back under the covers. All he could achieve was a half-sleep, half-awake limbo of unsettled disquietude. He drifted, pushing today's events from his mind as best he could, sinking so slowly toward wished for oblivion but somehow bogged down with baggage he could neither jettison nor resolve.

It came to him (although this was not so) that he was wide awake, staring across the bed toward his feet (now uncovered from the tossing and turning). Staring out at the darkness in the room. The darkness began to brighten. At first it was a small oval of gray mist that expanded and lightened into a dim, hazy glow. The mist swirled, took on an indistinct form, a familiar shape but not one he readily identified. As the form began to solidify he saw that it was a human form; a man made out of something which ebbed and flowed like smoke. Now it was thick, like milk suspended in clear liquid. Now it was solid. A man, robed, turbaned, stood at the end of his bed, beckoning. Something was in his hand: a piece of paper. Jefferson tried to reach for it but he was paralyzed and could not move.

15

Battlefields

"These hallucinations are driving me fucking crazy!" Jefferson told Blount a number of days later at his next session. "I don't mind the dreams so much, but these waking daymares just make me think I'm looney-tunes."

"I could refer you to a colleague of mine who can write prescriptions. I could send your file to her and you probably wouldn't need to go to her for too many sessions. She can fix you up with something to get you through the night, if you know what I mean."

"I don't know. I've never been good with drugs. Got sick on pot if you can believe that."

"These kinds of drugs would have the opposite effect of pot. More or less stabilize you."

"I think I'll pass for now. Did I tell you about the ghost? The one at the foot of my bed?"

"A very common place for ghosts to appear. Usually it is someone recently deceased…a spouse or a child. A wishful vision. The beginning of grief…a manifestation of the denial state."

"Yeah, well I was at the opening for the photographs and I saw this guy's reflection in the glass over the photo of the Professor…you know, the one we thought we saw a ghost on. Anyway, this guy had a bandage on his head like he had taken a fall of some kind. Reminded me of the turban the ghost wore. It freaked me out. Later that night the Professor's ghost appeared to me…I guess in a dream…and you know what? He had this fellow's face! Same guy. And I had a premonition, if you can call it that, when I met the man, that he was going to die. At least I think that's what I felt."

"So did he?"

"Um, no. I don't think so."

"I don't have any more tests to put you through. I'm not entirely sure you fit the profile I need for my study, but I'm intrigued by your story. Would you do this for me? Keep a journal. Write down everything that relates to out-of-the-ordinary events in your life no matter how trivial it may seem. Even write down ordinary events if they seem at some point to have been significant. Come and see me in a month or so. You might be amazed at how journaling can help someone with your obvious issues of self."

"Issues of self?"

"Like trying to bite your own teeth, remember?"

"Tell me one thing, Doc. You and Betty. Anything there?"

"You don't need to call me 'Doc.' Just Rodney will do. And as for Betty Snyder, I helped her through a bad time when her husband was killed in the war."

"That's all?"

"That's all. You have my word on that. She's a sweet kid, but I never go beyond a professional relationship with my clients."

"How about *after* they are your clients?"

"Hmm. Come see me in a month. And have a heart to heart with Betty. I'm sure she needs you in her life."

She stood at the door but did not invite him in. There was a storm coming; wind rattled tree branches and sent little dust devils skipping along the avenue. A drop in pressure, a chill, a darkening, all the foreboding whispers of the approaching relentless shouting match nature was about to unleash. Betty's long thin dress blew against her legs, clung like a second skin.

"I'm sorry I doubted you. I was being a jealous fool," Jefferson began.

"You were being an idiot. I don't own you any fidelity…especially in the past tense. What my life has been like is not yours to criticize. What we are…or might be…is also not up to your discretion. It…if there was to be an it…would need to evolve naturally, with tenderness, trust, and understanding. You don't get me, Jefferson. Maybe you never will."

"I want you in my life, Betty. I need you to complete myself. I need to be important to you."

"That's easy for you to say. Did you get that from Rodney in one of your sessions? Is the old guru counseling the lovelorn on winning friends and influencing women?"

"I've hurt you. I'm sorry. What can I do?"

"Right now…nothing. Just go away for a while. Maybe in time…"

She closed the door and disappeared from Jefferson's view…maybe forever. The first blast of rain thundered down on Jefferson as he walked back to the car. He was instantly soaked but he barely noticed. He had left the windows down and the seat was dripping. He sat in a puddle of water as he drove back to the motel.

He stood on the crest of the hill, looking at the graves. There were two cemeteries here, the National Cemetery where Lincoln gave his famous address, and the older, Evergreen Cemetery that predated the Civil War. He chose the older site to photograph. He didn't want any Civil War soldiers creeping into his dreams tonight.

She had asked him to go; he was mortified thinking about how completely he had bungled things. He wished there was an open grave here where he could lie down and cover himself with soft, comforting earth. In the morning after their argument he had driven past her house, and then driven past it again, and driven past it one more time, but he hadn't stopped. He had packed up the Subaru and set out for the open road. It had taken him about two and a half hours to drive from Windber to Gettysburg, along Highway 30, through country that had not changed much since the days of William Penn.

Now he roamed the old cemetery, photographing and taking notes. He didn't have to brush aside twigs and branches to get a cleaner shot here; Evergreen Cemetery was spotlessly groomed. Today, perhaps because of the magnitude of solemnity he felt in this historic place, he had turned off the sound function of his camera. Each picture was a silent tribute to the past. And silence seemed not only appropriate but mandatory here where history reigned and monuments to heroism had been raised on sacred ground. Even the ghosts were silent.

Gettysburg had been a farming community before the war, attracting Scots-Irish immigrants and others. Its population had grown to 2,400 citizens by 1860. The town had the usual array of business enterprises: tanneries, carriage makers, taverns, shoe makers, dress shops, and a photography studio. Its cemetery, up on the ridge above town, had graves dating back to the 1700s. Its location, up on the ridge, had been selected for an artillery platform by the Union Army. Grave stones had been tipped over to make way for canon. Several of the larger monuments would be shattered by enemy fire in the ensuing battle for Cemetery Ridge.

There were some Civil War combatants buried here, although the neighboring National Cemetery, dedicated by Abraham Lincoln, was the official burial site for victims of the Gettysburg battlefields. There were even two Confederate grave markers at Evergreen. The significance of the battlefield was such that nearly every inch of it had been explored, details recorded, histories written, and photographs taken so that Jefferson now questioned his own willingness to labor at documentation—documentation that already existed, bound in the glossy covers of publications, posted on web sites. But something had drawn him to this place.

Here lay Peter Thorn (1826 – 1907) and his wife, Elizabeth (1832 – 1907). Following the battle, Elizabeth had dug graves in the rocky soil while being six months pregnant. She was renowned for her first-hand account of the battle. And there lay John Burns (1793 – 1872), a civilian who fought along side the Iron Brigade in McPherson's Woods, was wounded three times but lived to meet President Abraham Lincoln. And over here, a monument to Mary Virginia "Jennie" Wade (1843 – 1863), the only civilian killed at the battle of Gettysburg.

They were all at the McClennan house that morning: Jennie, her mother Mary, her brothers Sammy and Harry. Jennie's sister, Georgia McClennan had just given birth to a fine new son and the Wades were at the house helping to take care of Georgia and the new born infant. The Confederates had already invaded Gettysburg and the battle was raging nearby. Most of the townfolk had hidden in basements or evacuated the town. Jennie and her family went about their business even though there were skirmishes right around the house.

Jennie carried water to wounded Union soldiers in the yard, brought food and gave them what comfort she could. Mini balls struck the wooden siding of the building. She and her mother were in the kitchen, kneading the dough they would make into bread to feed the soldiers when an artillery shell hit the building, tearing a hole in the wall. Luckily, it did not explode. Jennie fainted at the impact. Now they would retreat into the basement.

In the evening, the Rebels attacked the Union artillery placement on Cemetery Ridge. The battle lasted through the night but finally the Confederates were routed. Jennie and her mother returned to the kitchen to continue making bread. It was about 9:00 PM when a Union soldier came to the door.

"Ma'am? Miss? Would you have any more bread? Our boys are hungry. Casin' them Rebs is mighty hard work."

"We're just making a new batch now," replied Mrs. Wade. "You just wait here. It'll be just a bit before it's baked properly."

The soldier slumped down against the outside wall. Jennie's mother returned to the kitchen.

"Mother," said Jennie, "we are running out of flour."

Confederate snipers were abroad in the town. They took notice of the fact that Union soldiers often came to the McClennan house for food. They waited for an opportunity to take down some of the enemy. They sometimes took pot shots at the house just for practice.

Morning, July 3, 1863. A soldier had come to the door asking for bread again They told him to come back later. The family had a merger breakfast. Then Jennie repaired to the north parlor and stretched out on a chaise longue, exhausted from constant work and worry. She picked up a bible, turned to Psalms and began reading aloud:

> *The LORD is my light and my salvation—*
> *whom shall I fear?*
> *The LORD is the stronghold of my life—*
> *of whom shall I be afraid?*
> *When the wicked advance against me*
> *to devour me,*
> *it is my enemies and my foes*
> *who will stumble and fall.*
> *Though an army besiege me,*
> *my heart will not fear;*
> *though war break out against me,*
> *even then I will be confident.*

"Oh, Jennie," cried her sister, Georgia, "please do not read those words right

now. They make me so dreadfully worrisome. I am so afraid."

"I just meant to be comforting, Georgia. I shall stop now."

Georgia curled up on a bed that had been laid in the parlor, her baby next to her. The child slept. A sweet sight, thought Jennie.

"Oh I hope," Jennie said, "if anyone in this house is to be killed today, that it should be me. Please, God, spare Georgia and her baby!"

Snipers opened fire toward the house. Bullets struck the building. One passed through the window, shattered the glass and bounced off the bedpost where Georgia and her baby lay. It hit the wall and rolled to a stop at the foot of the bed.

At 8:00 AM Jennie rose from the longue chair. "There is to be no rest for the weary," she thought to herself. She entered the kitchen to begin kneading dough for the bread. Her mother joined her. It was only a matter of half an hour before the women had rolled the dough out into a baking pan.

"Would you start the fire, Mother?" Jennie asked.

Shots had been heard sporadically all that morning. The house was often struck by musket shot but the hard wood had provided adequate protection—up until now. A bullet hit the back door and penetrated the thinner wood. It continued, passing through the door to the kitchen. Jennie suddenly dropped the pan she had been carrying and fell forward against a table, then slumped to the floor. Her mother gasped.

The bullet had had entered Jennie's body in her back, just below her right shoulder blade, had passed through her heart, and stopped in her corset. She lay now on the floor, white from spilled flour, a crimson pool spreading out from under her. Mrs. Wade walked into the next room where Georgia was nursing the baby.

"Georgia," she said, "your sister is dead."

16

Jefferson's Journal

May 18, 2008 — It's Sunday. People have the day off, I guess. Not me. I either work or I don't. Depends on how I'm feeling. Does that make me self-indulgent? Probably. But if I don't feel a sort of inspired enthusiasm for the task ahead I get sort of depressed. Maybe depressed isn't the right word. Dulled. Stupified. Stagnant. Paralyzed. Mind-fucked. I can't function without that little surge of energy that comes from the anticipation of discovery. What am I looking to discover? I don't know. Haven't found it yet though, have I?

May 19, 2008. Time to get off my duff. Head out. I strolled the Gettysburg Battlefield all day yesterday. Saw all the statues, the plaques. Worked the graveyard and fell into one of those clairvoyant things where I experienced the death of a young girl, killed by a sniper's bullet. The consequences of war—slaughter of the innocent. The consequences of an 80 percent ESP index.

Later. Motel outside of Lancaster. Drove here to Pennsylvania Dutch country. Poked around. Here is a rich, ample countryside of historical little towns, an abundance of old cemeteries. Tomorrow I'll head up toward Lititz. Moravian Cemetery up there. Ha. It's funny they call it Pennsylvania Dutch, when the immigrants were mostly from Germany. I guess people confused "Deutsche" with "Dutch." Should be some good opportunities to get some excellent scrapple. (I ate at a great place for breakfast…a diner outside of York called Lee's. The scrapple was good, the coffee strong, the atmosphere steamy and aromatic with bacon and hash browns frying on the grill. I could live here…right in the diner!)

May 20, 2008. I think about her all the time. I should have stayed. Tried harder. Maybe I should go back. It's not too late, is it?

Lititz. I read a little about the place on the internet last night. Town dates to 1756…named after a town in Bohemia where Protestants had settled in 1456, escaping religious persecution. The Moravian Church was founded then and there, and some of the movers and shakers of the new religious order migrated to the New World. For a long time only Moravians were permitted to live in the town and only members of the congregation could own their houses. The land was all owned by the Church. One of the early customs of the church was "the Love Feast." I pictured something from the 60s: hippies and what not, but that's not accurate, of course. Simply a sharing of food during the service. It sounded interesting though.

I'd look for graves with some of the names of the early settlers: Jacob Huber, Christian Bomberger, John George Klein, Samuel Ranck, George Eby, Valentine Grosh, Israel Erb. What would I find? Unreadable stones? Broken monuments covered with creeping vines? I read that the graveyard was enclosed by a white fence with three gates and a large stone arch. An avenue of cedar trees separated the resting places of the men from those of the women. Strange! The first person was buried there in 1758—right up my alley!

When I reached the cemetery it was, of course, immaculately maintained. Here was an older section, with graves laid out along a grid and stones laid flat on the ground. I did find markers for a few of those original settlers I mentioned. I learned a story later about one of the interred named Thomas Utley. Here I copy what I found on the internet:

An unmarried son of the Rev. Richard Utley, born in Bethlehem, June 27, 1751. Shoemaker. A consumptive, he came here in August, 1770, at the suggestion of Bro. Tobias Beckel, who was much attached to him, to have medical treatment from a certain Dr. Blank — "the old Swiss doctor" — who at that time practiced in this neighborhood. In connection with the burial of this Brother, the Brethren's House Diary gives us the following singular circumstance: When the gravedigger had partly filled in the grave he heard <u>three distinct knocks</u> which seemed to him to come <u>from the inside of the coffin-lid</u>. He quickly called a number of the brethren to the spot, and they decided to re-open the coffin, for if they failed to do so, an unfounded "talk" would be the result: therefore, it was *taken up and opened; but Brother Thomas lay just as he had been deposited there, and not a sign of vitality was apparent. The brethren inferred that the knockings, which were <u>heard again</u> as they re-filled the grave, arose from the pressure of ground on the coffin-lid.*

As I wandered through this part of the cemetery I happened to come across a man, most likely a caretaker, who saw my camera and inquired what my purpose might be. I explained I was a genealogical researcher wanting to record data on older sites. He said to me, "You want to see the first cemetery? It's off Broad and Vine Streets, not far from here."

I learned from the man that there had been an old log church there that the Moravians had called Saint John's Church. The old grave yard had been used from 1744 to 1791. In the late nineteenth century it had been renovated somewhat, having been found to be covered in brambles and the stones encrusted with mold. The church officials leveled the ground, re-laid the stones in nice straight lines, but in doing so, may have misplaced a few.

I hurried to the location, in the midst of modest residences and a few old barns repurposed as garages. Under the shelter of several ancient and towering cedars I found a small park-like area with the simplest of identifying features: a granite stone with a bronze plaque announcing that this was Saint John's Cemetery. This stood just behind a stop sign and adjacent to another sign warning dog walkers to please pick up their waste.

The stones were flush with the ground…all indicative of the attitude of the people buried there: "death levels all, great and small—we need no monuments to glorify our existence on earth (the glory awaits us in Heaven)"—or at least I so perceived from the peaceful simplicity of the place. I won't list here any of the names and dates I found…these are in my notes and will be transferred to my web site in due course. I'll mention just a few which captured my imagination (although I am happy to report I did *not* dream about them). I got this from the old church records:

Jacob _____, son of Jacob _____, Sr. Died 1749—was ten years old. He was exercising himself in jumping, at the same time holding an open knife in his hand. He fell upon it, the blade piercing his heart, and he died one minute later. Then there was John _____, died 1760, aged two years. Drowned in the Lititz creek on his father's farm adjoining the Lititz tract on the east. And Christian _____, died 1764, son of John _____. Met his death in falling from a tree. Thirteen years old.

Of course there were many, many infant deaths and people dying very young of small pox or consumption. But somehow I am fascinated by *accidental* death. Why? I don't know. But the more tragic the better. Not that I don't feel pity for the departed...

May 24, 2008. I haven't "journaled" for a few days. I felt I needed a break from all this death stalking and zipped down to Philly for a little R & R. Had to make the all the requisite stops: Reading Terminal Market for oysters, Geno's for a cheese steak (also Pat's across the street, but I liked Geno's the best), Bookbinders for crab cakes—you may think that all I do is eat and drink, and you'd be right. I did go to the Rodin Museum, although they wouldn't let me take any pictures and I had to check my camera (it looked "too professional"). Of course there are more diners than you can shake a stick at here. And pretzel venders on every corner.

Yesterday I woke early and decided to drive out to the neighborhood of Kingsessing. There is an old abandoned cemetery there...a "must see" for those of us who dabble in the morbidity of our civilization. I knew a little about it, and opted for my film camera instead of my digital one. Here I would be taking "art" pictures rather than those documenting the graves.

I parked in the lot off of Kingsessing Avenue: a gentle loop of an access road that didn't prepare the visitor for what lay ahead. It was a short walk to the gatehouse. Gatehouse! Some ancient ruin of Greece or Rome could not have been more decrepit, more decayed, more vine-covered from neglect and age-worn by relentless winters and blazing summers. And beyond—monuments which now hosted scraggly vegetation; saplings grown up through cracks in the stones as if they were ornate pots, albeit inscribed with epitaphs and mementos. A thick carpet of weed. Trees that seemed embarrassed to sprout from graves, their roots entwining the rotted caskets below.

This was Mount Moriah Cemetery, established in 1855. One of the largest tracts of land near Philadelphia devoted to the interment of the wealthy, the heros of war, victims of disease, infant deaths, old age—a virtual cityscape of monuments in a once pristine, landscaped setting that could revival Pere Lachaise in Paris or the New Burying

Ground in New Haven. So grand that Betsy Ross was buried here (although moved in 1976 for the bicentennial—a very wise move indeed!) Now obelisks are toppled, mausoleums are bricked up and decorated with graffiti, headstones are splintered by weather and plant life, poison ivy threatens would be preservationists who will come, one hopes, and undertake the monumental (no pun intended) task of stripping away the jungle, restoring the grandiose gatehouse, removing the trash, old tires and other junk left here by inconsiderate people who, nonetheless, were undeterred by the state of decrepitude of the surroundings.

Why the decay? This was a privately owned cemetery. Only a few years go, the last member of its board of directors died. Apparently, no one owns Mount Moriah now. Certainly, no one maintains it. No one but Mother Nature, who could care less about human propensities to mimic immortality by virtue of blocks of granite and sculptures of angels. Ah, Ozymandius, I have found a suitable resting place for you among these derelicts of time.

I am at first inclined to say how incredibly sad this place is. Pathetic might be a better word. But then I think about the real purpose of cemeteries…not just a storehouse for cadavers but a place for spectacle, for glorification, for the denial of ordinariness, the denial of membership in a race of mortals who, once struck down and riddled by worm and bug, are just as much dust as the next person. How elegant the casket, how intricate and expensive the marker…how dead you are. You tried to take it with you, didn't you?

And contrast this with the simple statement made by the stones in the Moravian Cemetery of Saint John's Church.

I need to go back to Windber. I need to see her again, plead my case. Life is too short to spend it alone among ghosts.

Byron Grush

17

The Return

Here I am again, he thought…standing at her door, knocking meekly, waiting for her to glare at me through the screen. At least it wasn't raining this time. He knocked, but forcefully. He could hear the cat mewing behind the closed door. At least somebody will be glad to see me, he thought. Then the door opened, also forcefully. She stood staring at him for a moment; how beautiful she is! She isn't smiling though, is she?

"Well, if it isn't Mr. Paranoia," she said.

"Paranoia is…"

"Yeah, I know. Paranoia is the spice of life."

"I was going to say, Paranoia is a unique insight into reality."

"Is that from some movie? Look, you better come in. I'll warn you, though, I'm still angry."

"I hadn't noticed."

Once they were seated in the front room, the cat rubbing against Jefferson's legs, the tension seemed to dissipate to a degree—a degree, Jefferson believed, which might enable them to have a normal conversation. Of course, what was normal about any of their conversations?

"I realize you probably aren't ready to take me back," Jefferson began. Brilliant opening, he thought. It presupposes that she *will* take me back sometime in the future. "I actually came to ask you for a tremendous favor. I've taken some photographs…good ones, with my film camera. Took them as Fine Photography (as that the correct term?) Anyway, I've given up on cemetery recording and I want to try making it as a photographer. A real photographer with a gallery and commissions. I stopped and picked up a developing tank and some chemicals I would need. Can I use your darkroom?"

"Why Jefferson, that's wonderful. I'm so glad you've given up photographing tombstones. What are your pictures of?"

"Tombstones."

Here, thought Jefferson, there should be a rim shot, a har-de-har. Or at least someone should say that *irony* was the spice of life. But Betty just stared at him.

"Really, he said, "it's a completely different thing. I found this old abandoned cemetery. The place was overgrown with all kinds of vegetation, vines, big trees. It was in ruins. That sort of inspired me. I approached it as if I were at some old Greek ruin. I could imagine sprites and vestal virgins running through the brush cashed by satyrs."

"No ghosts?"

"No ghosts."

"Well, let me think about it. I am glad you came, however. I want you to see something. Drive us over to the museum, will you?

"Of course. But what...?"

"You'll see in due time."

The banner had been taken down that had announced the show. It wasn't a Saturday or a Sunday, so they had the place to themselves. Betty led Jefferson into the room where the exhibition was still mounted on the walls. She took him to the photograph of the Professor. "What do you see?" she asked.

It had returned: the image of the turbaned man standing behind the table, hand out-stretched and still holding the piece of paper. It seemed more distinct this time. Still translucent, but details were more finely etched. The features of the man's face were clearer. He didn't look anything like that man, Mr. Tinsley, who Jefferson had mistaken for the ghost.

"Has anyone else seen this? Or is it just we who are crazy?"

"In fact, one of the museum visitors brought it to my attention. I rarely looked at that particular photograph. I guess I was a little scared the damn thing might start spewing ghosts out onto the floor or something. But I think you met him...Alan Tinsley? He was at the opening. Anyway, he came back to look at the show again and he pointed out the ghost image. It was very amusing, he said. Those Victorians really loved their Spiritualism, he said. Didn't for a minute think of it at a 'real' ghost, he said."

"Well that's a relief. We can't have too many people latching on to this thing…like they do with that haunted hotel. I think we should take the picture down for now."

Betty shook her head. "Yep, that's Mr. Paranoia all right!"

"Really, Betty. Of course, maybe you'd prefer to make postcards out of it and sell them in the museum."

"Jefferson! What a grand idea! I've been worrying about money lately. We need a fund-raising plan. I bet we could sell…not postcards…but prints of some of these photos. How would you like a job?"

"We'd need a better equipped darkroom. A print dryer. Alternately, we could just scan the plates, like I originally suggested, and make giclée prints. We could rent a good scanner and an ink jet printer. My laptop is pretty powerful."

"I have a computer, you know. But I like the idea of actual photographic prints."

"But not off the original plates. We'd have to make duplicate negatives. You'd gain some contrast and lose details. The computer idea is much more practical."

"Sounds like you're hooked, my love."

"Sounds like I am. Am I forgiven yet?"

"Not quite yet, but you're gaining on it."

"I do have a board of directors, you know," Betty explained. "They mostly leave me on my own. I guess they appreciate the promotions I do…like the photography show. But they control the budget. I've emailed them to request some funding to buy a scanner and printer. They'll be meeting tomorrow to discuss it."

Jefferson was inspecting the roll of developed negatives that hung in the makeshift darkroom to see if they were dry yet. "I'll need an enlarger to print these," he said. He also would need funding in order to pursue his new career as a photographer. He couldn't ask Betty to bankroll his endeavor; couldn't ask his parents who had their own problems trying to live on a fixed income; couldn't (probably) get a bank loan—maybe he should have stayed with digital photography. Silver-based film photography was an ancient art form, born in the 19th century (and died in the 21st).

"You know who is on the board of directors? Your Mr. Tinsley.

You never did apologize to him, did you? I hope he doesn't remember the slight. He is, I think, enthusiastic about the photographs. Perhaps he'll help."

"He was the man with the bandage on his head. Is he accident prone?"

"Now that you mention it, he broke his arm falling off a ladder last year. And the year before…"

"Is there a community college nearby? I bet they'd have a darkroom. I could take a class…hell, I could *teach* a class!"

"There is. In Johnstown. Next to the campus of U of Pittsburg, a pretty easy commute."

"Commute? From here, you mean? Or should I move there? Save some money."

"Jefferson…I know that motels are costing you money. When you moved in here with me it was cheaper, wasn't it? I don't know if I'm ready, but…"

"Hey, I don't have the job yet. We don't even know if they teach photography there, or if they need an instructor."

"Optimism is the *sweetener* of life. Think positively. About everything!"

The scanner and printer arrived. The board of directors had liked Betty's proposal so much they had agreed to upgrade the museum's computer as well. Betty set up a small production area in the museum's basement where she, with Jefferson's help, could scan the glass plates, work on them in Photoshop to control contrast and sharpness and maybe remove a few of their scratches and other blemishes.

The community college didn't offer courses in photography, although they did have a program in media as part of their journalism curriculum. Video. Ugh. His ambitions forced to the back burner, Jefferson immersed himself in the scanning project. He realized he could scan his own negatives, the one's he had taken at Mount Moriah, and make giclée prints with archival ink and fine paper. He wasn't thrilled with the idea, still being something of a purist when it came to silver-based photography, but even professional printing paper had changed, was no longer on a paper base. The control he wanted was more available in software programs like Photoshop—but was that cheating? He pictured himself as Ansel Adams, lugging a heavy field camera through the snow-bound Sierras, making only one or two exposures in an entire day. Get with the 21st century, Jefferson, he told himself. As the kids say, LOL!

The first trial prints of the glass plates came out rather nicely, he thought. He picked another glass plate at random and placed it on the scanner, lowered the lighted lid and when to the computer to scan a preview. It was one they hadn't printed before. A little too deteriorated. This would be an excellent test of the technology he was now using. He made a scan and looked at the results in Photoshop. A little tweaking here, a little enhancement there, selecting those areas that were like dark blotches and lightening them, selecting those areas that were too white (built up emulsion on the plate that held back the scanner's illumination) and working with them to bring out details, sharpen certain areas…

Was that lettering? It appeared someone had at one time written on the glass plate in an elegant 19th century long hand script. Reversed. No problem, flip the image on the screen. Rotate it. Yes, almost legible. Increase the magnification. Was it a signature? And under that, the name of a photography studio. Bingo! Now he knew where at least some of the photographs had been made.

18

The Photographer

It was a good location for a photographer's studio, up along Railroad Street in the Old Conemaugh Borough district of Greater Johnstown. There was a competing studio down by the end of the Franklin Street Bridge…those Caddy and Green fellows, but their proximity didn't worry him. It was a good thing to have similar businesses in the same neighborhood. People would shop, look in the windows at samples, and surely see that his product was superior! And people did come to Railroad Street to shop; there were groceries, a cobbler, a confection shop, hotels and saloons. Yes, Thomas and Son Fine Photographers would thrive here, just as his father's original daguerreotype business had thrived for all those years until his death in 1849.

The move to Railroad Street was a smart one, he thought. The old location had been too near the flood basin of the Conemaugh River, where Stonycreek and the Little Conemaugh merged. There were always occasional floods. He remembered being a boy of 12 and entering his father's studio to find several inches of water covering the floor. The old-timers said it was just a matter of time before the big one came…the one that would wash away all the sins and all the sinners of Johnstown. Well, old-timers were always complaining about something, always doomsaying, always trying to frighten little boys. Conemaugh was on high ground. It would take a flood of immense proportions to reach *his* door.

He had used the name "Thomas and Son" in part to honor his father, and in part to induce his father's old customers to come in for a modern portrait. At first he had adapted his father's old daguerreotype camera to accept the new colloidal wet plates, but newer lenses were much sharper, could work under lower lighting conditions, and came with mechanical shutters. He invested in a portrait camera that had interchangeable lens boards. He bought a standard portrait lens and one of those twin lens outfits that took stereopticon pictures. So far, he hadn't found much of a market for the stereos, but that would come, he was certain.

Gregory Chesterfield Thomas, Jr. had great prospects. He busied himself now, arranging some cabinet cards in the window. There was a group portrait of a wedding party—such a beautiful bride! And several full-length portraits of men and women standing or seated, in pairs or singly, against fanciful landscape backgrounds or heavy draperies. He was most proud of the one of two little girls, twins, their long hair loose and flowing across their shoulders, their flared dresses nearly reaching the floor, the toes of their shoes poking out from under their hems like curious mice. Someday he would try his hand at hand-coloring this one.

His specialty was the close-up. Head and shoulder portraits that clearly defined the character of the sitter. He had mastered a vignette effect where the subject seemed to float against a neutral background. Certainly this should be very popular, especially with younger people. Have your portrait taken in a vignette to give to your lover, your wife or husband, your parents.... Now all he needed was customers. He thought, perhaps I should take out an ad in the Mountain Echo...but the expense! He had spent all of his inheritance on camera and darkroom equipment.

The bell over the door of the shop jingled. Thomas turned to see a tall man, hatless (and in this weather!), his vest unbuttoned and his suit jacket thrown over his shoulder. Despite the coolness of the day the man was sweating. He must have been hurrying along the street, possibly even running. Curious. Thomas put down the last of the cabinet cards he was in the process of placing in the window and asked:

"With what may I assist you?"

The man was breathing hard. He struggled to say, "I'm sorry. I must look a fright. I'm in a tremendous hurry but I wanted to talk to you about doing some photography."

"Well, of course, that's my business. You've come to the right place. But won't you sit? Take a moment to catch your breath? My word, man, why in heaven's name were you hurrying so?"

"It's not important. Yes, I should sit down. Would you be so kind as to get me a glass of water?"

Thomas returned with a beaker brimming with fresh water. "Sorry," he said, "I have no drinking glasses here so I've used this measuring beaker. Don't worry though, it's been sufficiently rinsed."

The man gulped the water. "Thank you. I should introduce myself. My name is Alexander Cohn. Perhaps you've heard of me?"

"No, I'm afraid I haven't. Are you famous?"

"In some quarters. Mr. Thomas, may I ask you a personal question? I wish to inquire whether or not you believe in the afterlife."

"The afterlife? You mean like heaven and hell? Well, I am good church-goer, Mr. Cohn, and I do take to the notion of a just reward in the hereafter."

"But do you believe that the soul can remain after the death of the body? That the blessed departed can visit and talk to the living?"

"You mean ghosts? No, I don't believe in ghosts. No Sir!"

"Well, Mr. Thomas, you see…I do. In fact I am…what you called 'famous'…in the Spiritualism community. We help to connect people with their lost loved ones. I have a certain talent in that area of endeavor."

"You run…what do they call them? Séances. Table rapping and flying trumpets and so forth."

"Not quite so dramatic as that, but we do attempt to reach the dead through various means, one of them being through a spirit medium, that is, one who enters a trance state and allows the departed to speak through them."

"And you are one…a medium? What do you want with me, Mr. Cohn. A portrait? Or do you want me to photograph a ghost for you?"

"You've hit the nail on the head, Mr. Thomas. Smack dab on the noggin. You see, we encounter a lot of skepticism in our business. People need to see some proof of what we claim. Sometimes…you mentioned the trumpets…it is useful to employ certain…devices to reinforce the experience. I'm not saying we cheat. We just give the process a little help on occasion."

"But how can I photograph a ghost?"

"That, I am hoping, you will tell me. Are there not tricks you can play? Double exposures, and so forth?"

"You don't cheat but you want me to. I don't know, Mr.Cohn. I don't think I want to be involved in a scam like that."

"I can make it worth your while. Very, very worth your while."

Gregory Chesterfield Thomas, Jr. studied the upside down image on the ground glass. Abruptly he pulled his head from under the focusing cloth. "Move just slightly to your left," he told the man in front of the camera. He was carefully composing the frame so that his current subject, a man dressed in a white robe and turban, would not overlap the sitter Thomas would photograph at a later date, on the same plate. He would not develop the plate until after the second exposure, creating a double exposure in which a "ghost" would appear to be standing next to the sitter—one of Cohn's clients—who would be unaware of the subterfuge.

"That piece of paper in your hand, hold it outward, as if you are handing it to someone. That's it. A little higher, please. Good. Now hold that position."

Thomas exposed two plates. He always took more than one picture when doing portraits, so now he would have two prepared ghost plates with which to work. Satisfied that he had the images he would need, he dismissed the turbaned man, an actor Alexander Cohn had hired to play the ghost. He marked each plate on its light-proof holder with a small "X" so that he would be sure to reuse the right ones when Cohn's client came for his portrait sitting.

"What an interesting experience," said Mr. Turban. "Are you making a set of exotic travel pictures to sell? If so, wouldn't it have been better to have some sort of background...palm trees or something?"

The actor apparently wasn't in on the scam. Just as well, thought Thomas. He answered the man's question thus: "No, it will be a sort of montage once I'm finished. I can combine the elements later."

This seemed to satisfy the man who then went into the dressing room to change back into his street clothes. It was now late in the afternoon so once the actor had left, Thomas decided to close up for the rest of the day, perhaps to stop for a drink at one of the taverns up the street before returning home. He exited the side door of the studio and walked up the alley which offered him a shortcut to Murphy's. A good cold glass of beer would take his mind off the deceitful trick he would be playing on Cohn's client. Well, he needed the money.

Because he had not left by the front door, he missed noticing the commotion in the street, just a block away. An omnibus had run over a man and killed him. While this event was not commonplace, it did happen now and then, and it usually attracted a crowd of curious onlookers. Today it had not. Today nothing would draw Thomas' attention to the fact that the actor who he had just immortalized in undeveloped silver colloid now lay dead in the street, a tangled mess of bloodied flesh.

"Alexander Cohn sent me here to have my portrait taken," said the bearded man who had just entered Thomas' studio. "He is preparing an article for publication, he says, and he wants to include my picture. The article is about the séance he did for me to contact the spirit of my brother who was killed in India last year. Trampled by an elephant, poor lad. Well, Cohn seemed to have brought his spirit back…at least *someone* spoke to me through Cohn. I'm still a bit skeptical about the whole business. You know, when they ask for donations, it makes you a bit suspicious, doesn't it? But still, I *want* to believe."

"Please come in, Mr…"

"Jefferies. Alan Jefferies at you service. I believe Mr. Cohn will foot the bill for this sitting, by the way. Is that acceptable to you, Mr…"

"Thomas. Yes, I had a communication sent to me that you would be coming. It will be paid for, there is no worry about that. Come over here where I have a nice setup all ready for you. Sit in this chair."

"I would be very happy if you could supply me with a copy of the portrait. I could pay for the extra print."

The scam was working just the way Cohn had said it would. Thomas, although worried that the deception might one day be discovered and himself discredited, even persecuted, sighed a sigh of relief and went to work. He found the two plate holders with the "Xs" on them. He would be done with this unnerving business soon.

Later, however, when he inspected the developed plates, he could see only the image of a bearded man seated in a comfortable chair against a neutral background. *There was no double exposed image of a turbaned man on the plates!*

Byron Grush

19

Schrödinger's Cat

The day after Alan Tinsley died Jefferson decided it was time to see Rodney Blount again. Tinsley's death had shaken him. The poor man had been walking his dog, an overweight Staffordshire terrier named "Piggy," when the dog slipped out of his collar and ran into the street. Tinsley panicked, ran after Piggy and was struck by a speeding minibus driven by a teenager who was talking on his cell phone and failed to notice either the dog or the man. That night, Jefferson dreamed that the ghost of Alan Tinsley stood at the end of his bed. He held out a piece of paper which Jefferson immediately grabbed—this time he would at least learn the contents of the paper. It said, "The end is near." Jefferson woke with a start.

Jefferson had brought Rodney Blount up to date on his psychic and non-psychic adventures. Blount sat behind his desk, leaning on his elbows, holding his hands in front of his face almost as if in prayer; the fingers of each hand touching and tapping in an annoying parody of an actor playing Sherlock Holmes. All he could say was, "Interesting."

"Why am I connected to all these dead people? Why do they haunt me so? Do I need an exorcism?"

"I think not," replied Blount. "Have you ever heard of Schrödinger's cat?"

"Is that a character from 'Peanuts' or something?"

"It is (and here Blount clasped his hand tightly together into a ball) a thought experiment by the physicist Erwin Schrödinger to address certain issues related to interpretations of quantum mechanics."

"I had a best bud in high school who worked as a mechanic. A real grease monkey. He had a souped-up 58 Chevy that…"

"Can't you be serious for one moment? I'm trying to help you here."

"Okay. Okay. Quantum mechanics. Parallel universes and so forth."

"Sometimes, yes. It depends on your interpretation. As I was saying, Schrödinger proposed placing a cat in a steel chamber with a Geiger counter, and a small piece of radioactive substance which was slowly decaying. Once the atomic particles decayed, the Geiger counter would react and set off a relay which in turn would release a hammer which would smash a sealed flask of hydrocyanic acid. Now here is the paradox: at any given time, is the cat still alive? Or is he dead? The quantum theory states that the cat is both dead and alive at the same time. Einstein would later point out that no one would question the possible state of the cat even though it were not observed, yet the issue of *observation* was crucial to the experiment.

"Now there is one theory, the Copenhagen interpretation, which suggests the superimposition of alternate states, i.e., the quantum state, ceases and takes on one or the other of the possible realities *once it is observed*. Are you following me so far?"

"Oh, absolutely. Parallel universes…like I said."

"Ah! You are catching on. Another theory, the Many Worlds interpretation, says that of course the cat is both dead and alive *at the same time* before the box is opened. But both versions of the cat are in separate 'worlds' and are equally real. They cannot, however, interact with each other."

"And the observer?"

"Opens the box and sees a dead or an alive cat…and his reality link with the animal becomes the state of the cat, therefore ignoring the alternate. Of course, it is true that the cat, the box, and the observer all are quantum systems governed by the same rules, and therefore even the observer may exist in superimposed realities. Thus propounding the paradox."

"And this all relates to me how?"

"The Many Worlds theory suggests that there is an infinite number of universes where everything that could possibly have happened in our past, but did not, happened in the past of some other universe. But these universes do not communicate. They do, however branch off from one another so that many possible paths may be followed. Your ghosts do exist on another plane and are superimposed in time-space with your reality. How you communicate with them is a mystery which probably violates the laws of quantum physics."

"Which means?"

"You need an exorcism."

As Jefferson came away from the session he found the words to a Willie Nelson song running through his head; like a lot of tunes that haunt you, this one would be hard to shake off:

I'm my own grandpa
I'm my own grandpa
It sounds funny I know
But it really is so
I'm my own grandpa

"Why are you looking at Bartholomew that way?" Betty asked Jefferson, who was staring at the cat with a (she thought) peculiar look in his eye.

"Just wondering about what size box he would fit in. And where I can get a Geiger counter. Oh, sorry…I'm a bit distracted today. You know, honestly, whenever I talk to Blount I come away more confused that before."

"Did I ever tell you about the so-called date we went on? You were pretty interested in our relationship at one time."

"I'm over that, but if you feel you want to talk about the man, I'm happy to listen."

"It was back in March. He took me to Philadelphia for the day. Very romantic…we went to a political rally."

"You saw Obama? I was there too! What a world!"

"It was a big crowd. And we didn't know each other then, did we? But wasn't he wonderful?"

"For some reason I would have thought you'd be rooting for Hillary Clinton. First woman president and all that."

"I was, before I heard that speech of Obama's. When he said 'race isn't an issue we can afford to ignore right now'…and that 'the legacy of discrimination is real and must be addressed'…that we had an opportunity now to really 'form a more perfect union'…those words resonated with me. Yes, I'd like to see a woman president. But I'd also like to see a Black man as president. I hope he wins the nomination."

"Well, you know I've said I'm not political. I'm a cynical, disenchanted, disenfranchised misanthrope who hates the whole system. But, I have to agree, that speech was riveting. I think I'll actually vote for him in the primary. Between the two of us, maybe we can swing it for him."

"You're funny. Just stop talking about putting Bartholomew in a box."

"Betty. Let's get married."

"No! Not now."

"Tomorrow then."

"Jeff…no."

"Then the day after?"

* * *

They had stayed up to watch the results of the 2008 presidential election. Their man had won! Barack Obama was now the 44th President of the United States! He had inherited two wars, a record deficit, a failing economy, a burst real estate bubble, a Wall Street bail-out and a congress full of Republicans who vowed to oppose him on every issue. Would he ever be able to overcome these enormous odds? Yes, he would.

Jefferson lay awake staring at the ceiling. Betty was sleeping next to him, her light breathing the only sound. He was happy—more happy than he had been in a long time. He had a beautiful wife; he had a beautiful house—well, *she* had a beautiful house and he lived in it; he had his own business, a photography studio where he snapped portraits of pimply-faced high school kids in graduation caps and robes or smiling middle-aged women whose head-and-shoulder shots would need some Photoshop touch up, and even dogs—cute Labradoodle puppies with red ribbons around their necks. Not the artist's life he had imagined for himself, but he was happy.

He couldn't sleep but felt himself sinking into that half-awake state, that limbo where the more he told himself to sleep the harder that was to achieve. Then he began to relax his body, relax his mind.

His breathing slowed, became deep. He was drifting, not into slumber, but in his mind; and this was accompanied by a bodily sensation of floating as if on a vast ocean whose gentle waves rolled and lifted him.

There was light although it was night. Light that seemed to issue from a thick mist that surrounded him, filled the room and obscured all the objects in it. The ocean on which he floated was composed of this same mist, liquid air not quite the consistency of water but of an ethereal substance that buoyed him upward, ever upward, into an empty, endless expanse where directions had no meaning and gravity had ceased to exist.

He hovered. If he looked down, would see his own body? Had he died? Was he now like Schrödinger's cat—existing simultaneously in two separate planes of reality—dead in one and alive in the other? Was he ascending to heaven? Would he see angels dressed in white robes, their wings folded against their backs? More then likely it would be devils...red devils with horns and pointed tails carrying pitch forks. Would there be any scrapple in heaven?

Or was he rising through the series of concentric planes of existence of the Spiritualists? Struggling from one plane to the next on a journey toward God? If he turned around could he climb backwards toward the first world where the living still waited? Could he enter into a picture frame or materialize as a jellied blob of ectoplasm?

Or perhaps he was in Chikhai Bardo, that fourth stage of the transmigration of the breath of life when it is just on the verge of death; next would come visions of the clearest light, the most perfect peace, the greatest awareness; then would come reborn consciousness according to whatever karma he had stored up in his former life. What karma did he have? Would he come back as a worm? A conqueror worm content to burrow through the rotting flesh and membranes of the empty shells of others? No doubt.

Still he floated. Neither up nor down. He tried to move his arms, his legs, but a sort of paralysis held him immobile. There was no fear attached to this, not the kind of fear one has when dreaming of premature burial, enclosed tightly in a wooden coffin, the realization that *you can never move again*. No, it was more like enclosure in the soft, nurturing womb of the mother where breath was unnecessary and a blessed symphony of pulsing fluids sang you into your first dream—a dream of the future. A dream of reentry.

Jefferson, Jefferson, what will they put on your tombstone? Gone, but not forgotten—he hath awakened from the dream of life—tears are often the telescope by which men see far into heaven—dust thou art, to dust returnest, was not spoken of the soul (Longfellow said that)—where there is much light, the shadows are deepest (Goethe said that)—good night sweet prince, and a flight of angels sing to thy rest (this one was on Douglas Fairbanks Sr.'s marker)—steel true, blade straight (on Sir Arthur Conan Doyle's)—that's all folks! (Mel Blank).

20

Death, Where is Thy Sting?

Oh he was dead all right. Deader than the proverbial doornail. It wasn't at all what he had expected. He floated. He could look down at his earthly shell, lying all scrunched up pretzel-like next to Betty. She would wake in a few hours, roll out of bed carefully to let him sleep while she made coffee, toasted bagels, stuck a pan of bacon under the broiler. She wouldn't yet know that his sleep was the endless sleep, the eternal repose, the ultimate cessation of pain, suffering, tedium, summer colds, and the winter heebie-jeebies. She would return to the bedroom followed by a waft of bacon-coffee-bagel fragrance. She would poke him, shake him—back away startled, incredulous. Freaked out.

By that time he would have drifted away through the ether toward his personal idea of the Bardo Plane. He would mingle with other earth-bound ethereal entities: the ghosts he had known by their epitaphs or their shadow images caught by camera lens and silver nitrate. They would take him on a tour of that pierced veil between the now and the never. They would show him the ropes.

But wait…is it possible he is only dead in one universe while still alive in another? Can he be really dead if he hasn't been *observed* as such—like that cat?

He had drifted up through the ceiling, through the roof, and into the night sky. He wouldn't be around to watch as Betty discovered his demise…it was just as well. He had no sadness for himself, but to see Betty in shock and grief would be unbearable. He thought…but it wasn't actually thinking, was it? For it didn't involve brain cells, the old gray matter. It was more of an awareness, or perhaps an absorption of idea as if through osmosis. He thought (it was the only word he could use to describe the process) that he had never before seen the night sky in such clarity. The brilliance of that star-flecked void…no, void implied emptiness. Expanse. Immensity. Infinite magnitude. He was star dust returning to star dust. His non-body emitted an answering brilliance.

Betty rolled over on her back and forced open her eyes. She wasn't quite awake yet. At least Jefferson wasn't snoring as he often did just when she woke and wanted a few more minutes of slumber. This morning, though, she wanted to get an early start; people were coming to the museum who were potential donors and a personalized tour was in order. One given with a contented smile, not with a grouchy frown left over from too much sleep and a rush through breakfast. She eased from under the sheet and blanket, set bare feet on the wood floor, and tip-toed from the bedroom, letting Jefferson continue sleeping. Usually he was a light sleeper but for some reason today, he was dead to the world.

A light breakfast of toast and coffee. Betty dressed, selecting a patterned blouse to go with a long, flowing skirt. Why be stuffy when the museum would be dingy enough on this bright, promising winter day? She glanced over at Jefferson, still huddled under the covers, a smile on his face. Let him sleep, she thought. After all, it *is* Saturday. She had to work but he did not. She would walk to the museum; there had been a light snow which covered the lawns and roof tops with a thin frosting that shimmered in the morning sunlight—the sidewalks were relatively clear.

Sally Pleasant was waiting at the museum when Betty arrived. She was laying out brochures on the counter at the museum's entrance. Sometimes Sally proved to be efficient and self-motivated. Other times she could be lazy and self-absorbed, satisfied to parade around in nineteenth century costumes garnering attention from visitors but taking little responsibility in the promotion of the museum. Today Betty was happy to have her help, however.

"When do the bigwigs arrive?" Sally asked.

"I'll be showing them around today, Sally. Just do your usual thing: stand there and look pretty."

"I contribute more than…"

"I'm sorry. Yes, of course you do. It's just that these are important, in other words, *rich* people and I want to make the absolute best impression on them."

The bigwigs were a wealthy couple from Johnstown, Mr. and Mrs. Everett Prendergast. The Prendergasts were major donors to the Johnstown Flood Museum and were in the process of establishing the Everett and Priscilla Prendergast Heritage Center in that same town. The Center would focus on the immigrant experience in America, with an emphasis on the colonial struggles of Western Pennsylvania—the hardships of the early settlers, their conflicts with the indigenous peoples they were supplanting, their achievements in farming the inhospitable landscape. Betty sensed the importance of establishing a good relationship with the Prendergasts, whether they donated money to her museum or not.

Sally Pleasant's family had been transplanted from the Deep South, to wit, the outskirts of Baton Rouge, Louisiana. Their migration had coincided with economic downturns in that region, Father Pleasant finding job opportunities lacking. Sally remembered playing under huge Cyprus trees dripping with Spanish moss. She remembered being heartbroken when the family moved—school friends lost and forgotten, barefoot strolls up dirt roads a thing of the past, smirks and laughter at her accent by the children in her new school. She was still a southern girl at heart.

Thus it was that the conversation Sally was having with Everett Prendergast—the one Betty had hoped to avoid—wasn't going to bode well for the museum. Betty had been in the kitchen arranging cookies on a plate. The snickerdoodles and the chocolate chips were a momentary distraction resulting in the suspension of her vigilance at the front entrance where she had hoped to intercept the Prendergasts. Sally, who was supposed to be attending to other patrons, seized on the opportunity to engage the illustrious visitors in a dangerous dialogue of a political nature. Betty cringed at the words "President Elect" which she heard upon returning to the museum entrance.

"People of good authority," Sally was saying to Everett

Prendergast, "maintain that he wasn't born in this country. It isn't legal for him to be president."

"Young lady," Prendergast returned, "I'm just glad you aren't of voting age yet. You still have time to get an education so that you won't believe all the clap-trap spewed out by sore losers."

"But I…"

"Sally!" Betty interjected. Don't you have some chores to do in the kitchen? Bring in that plate of cookies, please. And allow me to show the Prendergasts around."

Sally stomped out of the room. Betty turned back to the man once she was certain the girl was out of earshot. "Please let me apologize for our help," she said. "Sometimes I think she hasn't a clue to what reality is all about."

"Thank you for saying so. You know, I believe Obama is going to have a very hard time in the next eight years."

"No, thank *you* for saying 'eight years,' I do so hope this country comes to its senses. Finally we have an intelligent, honest, well-meaning man in the White House."

"Well, we all need our heroes. Mine was JFK. Um…I understand you have some interesting exhibits. Maybe we should get started?"

Betty escorted the Prendergasts throughout the first floor rooms with their glass cases filled with artifacts and then took them upstairs where the more permanent exhibits were laid out to represent a living room and two bedrooms of the 19th century. A long hallway led from the stairs and its walls had been appropriated for the display of the framed photographs that she and Jefferson had worked so hard to produce. Betty pointed these out, omitting any mention of the (was it controversial?) photo of the Professor and his ghost. In fact, she hurried the couple past that print feeling a sort of apprehension about it…not justified by any logic she could muster, but she was wary of it all the same.

After they had viewed the second floor rooms and presented Betty with compliments, and a few minor suggestions (that pillowcase is a reproduction, isn't it?), they retuned to the hallway. Betty stopped short when she saw a man standing in front of the Professor's picture, looking at it. When he turned she did not recognize him immediately…there was something different about him. But then:

"Jefferson! I didn't expect you to be here today, but it was nice of

118

you to come."

Jefferson said nothing, he only stood, staring at a space slightly over her head, as if he couldn't see her clearly.

"Jeffy, you look…pale. Are you feeling well?"

Betty turned to the Prendergasts in order to introduce Jefferson to them. Everett Prendergast looked very confused. "Who are you talking to?" he asked.

"Why…my husband. He…" But when she turned back toward Jefferson, he was no longer in the hallway. "That's funny. I thought I saw…"

They call it being "shocked." It isn't exactly the same as sticking your finger into a light socket, the electric vibrations traveling up your hand and across your arm, the involuntary shaking after pulling free from the socket—but it is similar. It is a mental state that paralyzes the brain, causes the breath to come in short, struggling gasps. Then inescapable reality arrives to chase away the disbelief. Shock. Oh no! Oh my God! It can't be.

But it is. It is your husband lying on the bed, rigor mortis turning that pleasant smile you saw this morning into a grotesque crescent of white teeth like neatly arranged miniature grave stones. The empty stare. The pasty pallor. The impossible gesture of the body like some dried up sea creature thrown upon the shore by the crashing waves. Yes, Betty, it is impossible. But true.

Bartholomew, the cat, won't enter the room. Hair bristles upon his back. The heat is stifling in the small bedroom, and the odor of death is apparent. She rushes to open a window: let death escape into the wintery evening. She gazes up into the darkening sky; no stars are out. She can't cry: that too is impossible. She turns back toward the bed and its ugly cargo. No. No, no no! She runs from the room.

*   *   *

"What was Daddy like?" six-year old Victoria asks her mother. She has accompanied Betty to the cemetery often. It has been strange for her to think of her father lying beneath six feet of dirt; the only image of him she will remember will be this polished granite marker.

"He was a good man, a kind man, a bit obsessed at times, but creative and talented. I never got to say goodbye…didn't have a

chance to tell him you were on the way. I miss him so much!" —
Tears.

Autumn days like today make visiting the cemetery almost
bearable. Leaves blowing like dead butterflies, their colors muting as
they dry. Jefferson would have liked spending eternity here...did like
it. For Betty always feels his presence here. Feels he is watching.
Believes that someday his ghostly manifestation will appear to her. If
anybody could return from the dead it would be Jefferson.

He watches but does not materialize. He isn't that kind of a
ghost. There is just too much of a separation between the universe he
inhabits and the one he had left. He marvels at his daughter, Victoria.
A real beauty like her mother. One day would she grow up to be the
second or third woman to become president? Would she become a
famous opera singer or a gifted scientist? Jefferson is in no hurry to
find out. It will be enough to watch her grow and mature...not as
satisfying as it would have been had he not died. But he will watch
these two women as they travel through their lives. He will meet
them on the other side some day.

About the Author

Byron Grush was born and raised in Naperville, Illinois, just southwest of Chicago. He is a third generation native of that town. Grush studied art and design at the University of Illinois and filmmaking at the School of the Art Institute of Chicago. At the Art Institute he was a student of Gregory Markopoulos, one of the originators of the New America Cinema movement in the 1960s.

Grush then taught at The School of the Art Institute of Chicago, creating a course in film animation in the mid-seventies. He later became an Associate Professor at the College of Art at Northern Illinois University in Dekalb, Illinois, where he taught in the Electronic Media area. He is the author of a book on hand-drawn animation techniques entitled *The Shoestring Animator*. Becoming interested in genealogy, he wrote a trilogy of historical novels based upon what he had learned about his early ancestors.

He and his wife moved to New Mexico in the late 1990s, and opened an art gallery featuring Outsider and Visionary Art in Santa Fe. They returned to the Midwest to retire in the small town of Delavan, Wisconsin, a place that reminds them of their roots. Grush writes, paints and studies Tai Chi.

Other fiction by Byron Grush

All The Way By Water
In which Isaac Grosh brings his wife and eight children to Illinois, traveling by flatboat on the Ohio and Mississippi Rivers.

Once Upon a Gold Rush
In which John and James Grosh journey by wagon train to California during the gold rush of '49. Introduces the characters of White Cloud and Little Wind.

Road of Stars
In which White Cloud searches for his father (James Grosh) and helps to build the Transcontinental Railroad.

Dance Beneath A Diamond Sky
This historical novel of the Sixties follows a group of young people as they search for identity, love, honor and redemption during the decade or so between the assassination of President John F. Kennedy and the resignation of Richard Nixon.

Violet at The Breakers: a novella
Violet might only have been twelve, but she was worldly. When her mother brought her and her sisters to Palm Beach, she hadn't expected to discover the body of a murdered man, or to be pursued by his killer. Nor had she expected a certain lady would be careless with a curling iron...

The New Unwritten Law: a novella
"The murder victim is slumped over his desk, a bullet hole in his forehead, a pool of blood spreading slowly on the green felt blotter on which he lies. The only door to the room is locked and bolted from the inside..." thus began the narrative presented as an intellectual puzzle by my friend and companion, Rodney Morton. What I didn't expect was that the game would be interrupted by a real-life murder—one that involved a former girl friend and her family. Now I had two mysteries to unravel.

Romeo's Revenge and Other Wisconsin Stories
An anthology of twelve short stories about the towns and people of Wisconsin.